MY
DEAR
YOU

Also by Rachel Khong

Real Americans
Goodbye, Vitamin

MY DEAR YOU

RACHEL KHONG

HUTCHINSON
HEINEMANN

HUTCHINSON HEINEMANN

UK | USA | Canada | Ireland | Australia
India | New Zealand | South Africa

Hutchinson Heinemann is part of the Penguin Random House group of companies
whose addresses can be found at global.penguinrandomhouse.com

Penguin Random House UK,
One Embassy Gardens, 8 Viaduct Gardens, London SW11 7BW

penguin.co.uk

First published in the US by Alfred A. Knopf,
a division of Penguin Random House LLC, New York 2026
First published in the UK by Hutchinson Heinemann 2026
001

Copyright © Rachel Khong, 2026

The moral right of the author has been asserted

Penguin Random House values and supports copyright. Copyright fuels creativity, encourages diverse voices, promotes freedom of expression and supports a vibrant culture. Thank you for purchasing an authorised edition of this book and for respecting intellectual property laws by not reproducing, scanning or distributing any part of it by any means without permission. You are supporting authors and enabling Penguin Random House to continue to publish books for everyone. No part of this book may be used or reproduced in any manner for the purpose of training artificial intelligence technologies or systems. In accordance with Article 4(3) of the DSM Directive 2019/790, Penguin Random House expressly reserves this work from the text and data mining exception.

Some stories were previously published in *Cut* (online version), *Freeman's*, *Guernica*, *n+1*, *One Story*, *Paris Review*, *Ploughshares* and *Tin House*.

Printed and bound in Great Britain by Clays Ltd, Elcograf S.p.A.

The authorised representative in the EEA is Penguin Random House Ireland,
Morrison Chambers, 32 Nassau Street, Dublin D02 YH68

A CIP catalogue record for this book is available from the British Library

ISBN: 978–1–529–15536–5

Penguin Random House is committed to a sustainable future
for our business, our readers and our planet. This book is made
from Forest Stewardship Council® certified paper.

For Eli

contents

My Dear You
1

The Freshening
15

Slow and Steady
37

Tapetum Lucidum
47

The Family O
73

Serene
105

Red Shoes
133

Good Spirits
155

Colors from Elsewhere
177

D Day
199

Acknowledgments
221

MY DEAR YOU

I selected fifty-four millimeters for the space between my eyes. All my life, my eyes had been far apart. Growing up, the other kids called me "Hammerhead." Something nobody tells you is that when you die a death in which your face and body are utterly maimed, you get to choose your face in heaven. Your body, to some extent, as well, because you're given a body that corresponds to your chosen face. But skin color, nose shape, lips, and teeth—it's all up to you. That's the silver lining.

"Take your time," said Richard, whose position or rank was I don't know what. I thought of him as my prison guard, even though this was, I was pretty positive, heaven. He spoke in short, authoritative sentences, and seemed bored, like prison guards on TV. It was just how I thought of him—I'm not saying that's what he was.

We'd been vacationing in Australia, Adam and I. It was a crocodile who murdered me, who clamped on my face and body with its many sharp teeth, and crushed my bones. It didn't chew me. That's not what they do. They swallow prey whole and grind up their food with countless little rocks in their digestive tracts. If the prey is too big to swallow whole, they tear it into smaller pieces first. The tearing and the rocks left my face entirely fucked. "Crocodile tears" are insincere tears because crocodiles cry when devouring their prey. Did this one cry when it ate me? They told me yes, because that's just what their glands do. How old was it? They told me seventy, meaning that this crocodile outlived me by forty years, which I didn't know whether to feel happy or sad about. Was it a male or a female? They told me a female. So really I got my life ended by an old crocodile bitch—though they're not called bitches but cows.

I asked Richard how much time I had to mull over the face and body parts they were permitting me to do over. He said twenty-four hours, but that heaven hours worked a little differently.

"Why, do you need an extension," he said without inflection.

I said no, it was okay. Richard had been so patient and accommodating with the questions I'd had so far, I didn't really want to impose further.

"How does this work?" I asked him.

"What do you mean?"

I wanted to know what the face would be *for*. Would I be eating with my new mouth? Would I be tanning with my new skin? And, another question I had, was there the possibility of ever falling in love again?

He said yes to all of the above, and that I would soon see that death wasn't so different from "life"—he used scare quotes—except for the new people. New-to-*me* people. I saw David Bowie ride by on a bicycle just then. But was it David Bowie or someone who'd chosen his face? Richard wasn't sure.

I chose brownish-green eyes with speckles. There was a computer program for this. All I had to do was drop the features into a shopping-cart-type basket, as though I were online shopping, and it would show up more or less instantaneously on my face, which I could then check the fit of right away in the mirror. I chose my original style of ears, a lightbulb shape, with soft lobes with a peachy fuzz. Adam had liked them. In our hotel room the night before the accident I had polled him on what he liked best about me. We were on our honeymoon, if you can believe. Earlobes, wrist, smile, he'd said, flashing me his cheesy one. I didn't have a strong opinion about ears, it turned out. They all looked serviceable to me. So I just picked my old ones but made them stick out less. I'd never liked my teeth so I changed those, too. I made them slightly bigger and whiter and more rectangular. Adam would've hated this, but he wasn't here, was he? We were thirty years old and had just promised, beneath a gazebo, in front of most of the people we cared about, that we would spend the rest of our lives together. And it was true that I did, I kept my part of the promise.

I wasn't sure if I wanted to be Chinese again, so I saved that detail for last. It felt unethical to get to choose. I closed my eyes and clicked the mouse to let the program decide. *Chinese*, it said, and my eyes sharpened at the edges, into the almond-shaped ones I'd had in life. I would be lying if I said I wasn't a little disappointed.

What Richard had meant about time being weird was that you felt it differently. One day I was playing racquetball with my new friend Heidi, and we were having a blast, swatting maniacally, unsure how to play because we'd never played before. Then we heard angry knocks at the door. It was a couple, holding racquets and looking testy.

"Can we PLEASE use the room," the woman said. "We've been waiting."

She had thick eyebrows that she raised at me, and no visible cheekbones. It was clear that this had been her face in life and that she had lost her life peacefully, perhaps in her sleep, or to cancer, which is not peaceful, I don't mean to offend, but you know what I mean. The man stared too long at me, at my perfect features.

"We're so sorry," Heidi said, deferring in her Southern drawl.

When we checked our watches we realized we'd been in there for four months.

As the time passed I could picture faces from life less vividly. My mother's was the first to go, then my father's—even though I'd seen their faces for thirty years, even though I would have said to you that I knew their faces intimately, almost as intimately as I knew my own face, which I began to forget as well. Troublingly, my boss's smug face remained clear. The other copywriters and I, we lived in constant fear. He was what you would call a "Toxic Boss." I once read an article about types of bosses—"the Micromanager," "the Inappropriate Buddy," and so forth. I recognized ours as a blend of "the Tyrant" and "the Incompetent"—slightly Machiavellian, though not intelligent enough to be fully so. If you had an idea you wanted implemented, you had to convince him it was his idea. We wrote copy for a few products: Reddish Fish, a knockoff Swedish Fish. A special kind of antibacterial athletic sock. I remembered the companies and I could no longer remember my parents' faces.

In the beginning here, I would see a man and think to myself, *His chin looks like Adam's* or *His hands, with their big rectangular nails, look like Adam's*. But after a decade I couldn't remember those hands, or his chest, or even his height. Was he tall? Was he short? I held as tightly as I could to the memory of Adam's face. Every morning I reconstructed him from the facts I clung to. The color of his eyes: hazel. The color of his hair: dark brown. The length of his eyelashes: long. His body was gone and his scent was gone, but his face I had, and kept, and I swore I'd keep forever.

Maybe it was an unhealthy fixation, but he *was* the love of my life.

~~~

Everyone in heaven is thirty-three years old, like Jesus. I was aged three years, and babies get aged a lot of years. Old men and women get years shed from them, but retain their emotional IQs and their years of life experience.

I know what you're wondering, and the answer is yes: people in heaven are smoking hot. Thirty-three is a hot age to be, especially when you've got the wisdom of an eighty-five-year-old. And, as you'd expect, octogenarians with thirty-three-year-old bodies are a little . . . well, let's just say they have one thing on their minds.

Sex wasn't what I was here for, of course. I mean, not that I was here for any particular reason. I was just going to be here, so I had to make the best of the situation. Not having to work at the agency was nice. I'd pick up some new hobbies, I thought, I joined a book club. I took a drawing class, mostly so I could draw faces, including you-know-whose. After about twenty years my racquetball skills turned a corner and I began beating Heidi, to both of our surprises. I enjoyed, for the first time in my "life," a fit, athletic physique. Not that my heart could give out, not that cardiovascular health mattered. But my new body looked good—for a while, anyway, until it was no longer novel.

Day in and day out I tried to remember facts about my former husband, the kaleidoscopic eyes and brown hair and long eyelashes. I drew his face over and over in my class, though it never looked completely right. And what was his name? Sometimes I couldn't recall and would have to check. *Adam*, I wrote in tiny, nearly imperceptible letters on my bedroom wall, but the janitor kept erasing it, and so I wrote it, *Adam*, on a scrap of paper, and tucked it underneath my fitted sheet, and remembered to retrieve it before every laundry day, which was Tuesday.

We had had our problems, Adam and I. Of course we did. We respected each other, though, and that, to me, was the main thing. We talked through our differences. The conversations were always helpful, but in my mind, they reinforced how separate we were. The day we got married I caught, in his eye, a glimmer of worry about what we were about to embark upon. That glimmer was like a shard of glass that flew over to me and caught on me like pantyhose to a dry patch of skin, like a burr to a sock, and I had to excuse myself from our table to cry in the expensive, carpeted Porta Potty.

"Tears of joy," I said when I returned, my face still wet, and Adam smiled and vacuumed the droplets off my cheeks with his mouth—a joke we had.

I constantly checked the paper under the mattress to remind myself of my husband's name. It was embarrassing how often I did this. I tried distracting myself with other activities: I played racquetball with Heidi, and sometimes we got brunch on weekends. I baked cakes for friends, experimenting with different recipes and alternative flours. I tried not to dwell, because I had tried that once, and as a result I spent a year just crying, which utterly wrecked my face, which took another year to unpuff.

What had my husband and I done together? I sometimes jotted things down, like a grocery list: I jump-started his car when he left the headlights on. He bit the backs of my knees in a playful manner. We watched streaming television. We had dinner with my immigrant parents, and his normal ones. We took selfies on our phones from crazy angles and sent them to each other, trying to outdo each other's hideousness. Before getting married we'd talked circles around marriage—what it would be, what it meant to people, was it a thing we were going to do? Sometimes the talks ended in me turning away, so my mouth could contort into a ridiculous down-turned shape, and I could cry quietly. There was never a warning: the sadness would overcome me all of a sudden. When we would each respond to something simple, like "How was your day?" or "How was work?," I would listen and wait for the truer answer: how he felt and what he was scared of, some insight into what one of his brain regions said to another of his brain regions. It was exhausting, I bet, for him. It was exhausting for me, too.

In the end, he was my husband for a day. Was I too

demanding? I just wanted to know him. I thought that was the point: knowing people. But what did I know, I guess, really?

On a Tuesday I was busy destroying Heidi at racquetball, and I forgot to hide the slip of paper that said *Adam* from the housekeeper, and when I got back, my sheets were freshly laundered and the slip of paper was gone. "Don't cry," I instructed myself, out loud, feeling myself about to. I called Heidi and we got drunk on artisanal gin and I didn't cry even though I couldn't believe it, couldn't believe what I had done. *You stupid, careless idiot,* I repeated to myself that night, incredibly drunk. *How could you?* And Heidi repeated Buddhist-type platitudes, like, *What's gone is gone.* She'd been a mom, and she'd had a heart attack at age fifty-six. She couldn't remember, any longer, how many children she'd had, let alone any facts about them.

"Where are you from?" people sometimes asked me, admiring my face.

"California," I would say.

"I mean, where are you from originally?" they would ask, and I would think, *Come on. Is this really still happening, here?*

I saw Richard from time to time at the grocery store. We would strike up light conversation. It turned out he wasn't my prison guard but just doing community service, volunteering with the new folks.

~~~

At the art studio where I was drawing what I could remember of my husband's face—which lately wasn't much, just that he *had* one, with all the regular stuff on it—a new guy was making a mug. He was stretching some clay into a handle.

"Who is that?" he asked, and though my husband's name was on the tip of my tongue, I couldn't recall it. It eluded me. "I'm sorry," he said, when he noticed how troubled I was not to know the answer.

"I'm Adam," he said.

"Hi, Adam," I said, liking the name, liking how it sounded when I said it. Adam asked did I want to have dinner sometime. I hesitated.

"I'm new here," he said, by way of explanation.

I almost said, "I'm new here, too," but in fact I'd been here for over fifty years.

We got burgers at the drive-in. We made small talk. He told me he'd died peacefully in his sleep. He was eighty-four. It was Christmas Eve. He'd been sick with pneumonia. His wife was asleep in the room; she'd been tending to him. He'd had a nice day with his daughters and son and their families. His was a pretty good one, he said, a little wistfully.

"Death?" I asked.

"I meant life," he said. "But yeah, that, too."

He asked some basic, new-to-death questions, like: Can I just eat whatever the hell I want without gaining weight? And: They do your laundry for you? (Answers: yes and yes.) He ordered a chocolate milkshake and chili-cheese fries, and wiped his greasy hands on his pants.

"Can you watch your family?" he asked. "Like, haunt them?"

And I said, "No, of course not." It was insensitive of me, I realized, when he seemed deflated. "I'm sorry," I added.

"It makes sense," he said.

Adam was easy to talk with. He cracked a lot of jokes, some that made me groan and a few that made me laugh like I hadn't laughed in years. He didn't ask me where I was from originally, or try to get into my pants. I have a hard time feeling comfortable with new people in general, but somehow he put me at ease. Depressing that that kind of person comes around only once every half a century, but again, I try not to dwell.

"You remind me of someone," he said. The word *remind* was practically foreign to me. I knew it meant something to some people, and I understood it in theory, but I couldn't put my finger on ever having been reminded.

"Could we do this again sometime?" he asked.

"Well," I said. "I'm kind of busy these days."

"I'm joking," I added quickly, when he looked disappointed again. "It was a joke! You'll get it soon."

"Tomorrow?"

"Sure, tomorrow."

He turned to go, then paused.

"Where are you from again?"

I held back a sigh.

"California," I said.

"But, like, where in California?" he asked.

"I don't remember," I said, honestly.

"Oh," he said. "Well, it's not important. See you tomorrow."

~~~

The next night we were supposed to meet at the clock tower. In the plaza, twelve Chinese ladies who vaguely resembled my mother were doing synchronized exercises. They were all my age even though I'm sure they had been one hundred when they died. Every night is a full-moon night, but the moon changes colors. Tonight it was lavender. Under the lavender moon the ladies glowed purple, and Adam circled them, in search of me, appearing nervous.

"Hey!" I shouted at him. Right away, his worried expression changed to a relieved one.

He held a paper bag containing two submarine sandwiches. They were cut in half, so we swapped halves and ate them on a bench by the river.

"I miss my wife," he said, softly. "I miss my kids."

"It's hard," I said, though I couldn't recall. Was it hard?

"It's hard," he agreed.

We stood to brush the crumbs off and began to stroll along the river. He hadn't finished his sandwich, so he clutched the paper bag as we walked. I wished I had something meaningful to tell him, in exchange for his sincerity. Earlier I'd beat Heidi in racquetball. I'd thrown a vase. My plan was to keep fresh flowers in the house more often, and the vase would hold them. I'd lifted my mattress and looked underneath, for some reason—I didn't know why.

I wanted to ask him more about his wife and his kids, but we were discouraged from encouraging nostalgia in new residents. What else could we talk about that would make us better friends and bring us closer? I racked my brain as we ambled.

A dog came up to us—a beautiful golden dog that was thirty-three in dog years, like all the dogs were. It was without an owner, without a collar. The dog allowed Adam to stroke its golden head, so I reached out to touch it, too. It stepped back. It looked at me and started to snarl, then bark. It was specifically barking at *me*. This was exasperating but familiar: this dog, unfortunately, was racist.

"There are racist dogs here?" Adam sounded skeptical.

I shrugged—disappointed but resigned. "There are racist dogs everywhere."

Adam reached into his paper bag and tore some meat from his sandwich. He gave the racist dog a little swatch of meat. The racist dog changed its tune. The racist dog was now *begging* us for more.

Adam handed me the sandwich bag, and I ripped off some meat, too. I kneeled to give it to the dog.

"Here, asshole," I whispered.

We fed the dog the rest of Adam's sandwich and started again on our way. The dancing women were no longer dancing, but chitchatting. The racist dog followed us. We would occasionally turn around to check if it was still there. It was.

"Maybe we should keep him," Adam said.

"Keep that racist dog?"

"He's reformed," Adam said. "He could make it up to you."

That had been my husband's strength, I suddenly recalled. He was good at soothing you, at the same time you weren't 100 percent positive that he really *got it*.

I took Adam's arm then. It was a beautiful night, the purple reflecting off the trees, off the water, off the houses. I fell a little bit in love, and then a lot.

"You have beautiful ears," he said, tucking my hair behind them, forgetting his wife already.

~~~

In the end we kept the dog. She turned out to be a she, and we named her Betsy and taught her how not to be racist, sexist, or bigoted in any way. Adam and I, we wound up being together for a hundred years, many of them great. We took Betsy for long walks, played doubles tennis, left our clothes at each other's places, made conversation topics of our fears. We were tolerant; this was love. Though the breakup was amicable, I cried and cried anyway, and he sucked each individual tear off my face like a vacuum.

"I've never seen you cry," I complained. "Not once in a hundred years."

And Adam looked into the distance, appeared to focus really hard, and squeezed a single tear out of the corner of his eye.

"Get a spoon," he said.

We slid the tear onto the spoon. Then he kissed me gently on the cheek, and was gone.

I used the spoon with the tear on it to stir sugar into my coffee, which is delicious here—it's the fairest of trade. I took my time drinking the coffee. It was heavenly: smooth and lacking any bitterness. It tasted like flowers and dirt. When I was finished, I put the mug in the sink, and even though we had custodians, I washed the mug and the spoon. While I was at it, I washed my face. I put my running shoes on, and my earbuds in my ears. I touched my toes to stretch. I jogged out of my house to pop music. Outside, it was a sunny day.

Here's what I know: Someone in my past mattered a lot to me. We had a beautiful, irreplaceable relationship that was one in a million. Sometimes I'll write them a letter. "My dear you," I'll start it.

THE FRESHENING

My cashier's black hair was beautiful. Though not unlike mine, it was shinier and thicker, and hung glamorously down to her waist. It looked strong, too, like Superman's in the Christopher Reeve movies. A strand of Superman's hair could hold up a thousand-pound weight. As a child, I watched those movies over and over: they were my favorite. Superman's hair, holding up the weight, looks as thick as a wire. A whole head of his hairs must have been heavy. But Superman's neck was so strong, I figured, the weight of his head didn't matter.

"Enjoy your last evening," my cashier said, adding "last" to distinguish this day, the same blithe way somebody might add "Happy holidays" to an email in December. With one hand, she flipped her lustrous hair off her shoulder.

She seemed youthful and careless. I guessed she was Filipina. She probably took her hair for granted, the way people in their twenties usually took their assets as givens. Then again, kids knew more these days.

She handed me my purchases in one bulging bag. I took

them from her. If I'd been bagging the items myself I would have given myself two double bags. But I thanked her, added, "You, too," and when she didn't look away from the next customer, I went on my way.

~~

At home, I removed the can of Pringles and one of the bottles of wine. I gave a cursory glance out the window to check for any neighbors—none—and pulled down my pants to stick a menstrual pad onto my underwear. I thumbed open the Pringles's plastic top, peeled off the foil, and got to work eating them.

When I was told by my mother's lawyer that she had left the house to me, my first thought had been that I would upgrade her full-size bed to a queen. I'm not proud of this, to have entertained this thought first, of all the possible thoughts. My second thought was that I was the worst. My third thought was not a thought at all but an overwhelming sadness. When I began to cry and found myself unable to stop, the lawyer had handed me a crumpled napkin from his pocket.

In life, my mother had not been unlike other immigrant mothers: demanding and exacting, unable to say the phrase *I love you.* Instead she talked about her immense sacrifice, how much she and my father had suffered to bring me to America, the land of opportunity, where everything turned out to be far more fucked up than she imagined. She never said "fucked up"—she didn't curse—but it was in the subtext. She'd tell me how impressive her salary had been back in Taiwan. Here, her looks and way of speaking had been held against her. In the first few years of living in America, she'd had to clean toilets and showers at a twenty-four-hour gym, where the muscled men would openly stare at her butt. She fumed in silence, but she didn't know enough English to ask them to stop.

Eventually, she lost her accent, and her English came to sound like any other American's. Yet sometimes, when she didn't want to be spoken to, she pretended not to understand. This was what people expected of an older Asian woman, so she played along.

My mother had been excited about the Freshening—the Identity Protection Act, as it was officially known. The trial runs had been positive—or positive enough. Now America, my mother felt, could truly be the land of opportunity. It was finally happening. Then she'd died—unfortunate timing.

I'd meant to drink the wine with the Pringles, but I got around to opening the wine only after I had eaten all the chips. I turned on the television and poured myself a glass to the rim.

A middle-aged woman reporter was at a college frat house, where bros in white-and-blue backward hats were partying. All across the country, people were celebrating the eve of the Freshening. They intended to stay up all night.

"It's, like, our Y2K," one bro said into the reporter's microphone. Behind him, three bros were shotgunning Natural Lights and surrounding bros were rooting them on. I tried to picture each of the bros as a distinct individual with his own hopes and dreams but, I'll be honest, I struggled to. It was a failure of my own imagination.

"We're witnessing history," another bro said. "I mean, it's pretty special."

We were each given a two-hour window in which the agents might come, like people installing Comcast, and mine was nine to eleven a.m. We were instructed to take the day off, but I would have been home anyway. I didn't work anymore. From my mother I had inherited enough to live on forever.

At ten exactly my doorbell rang.

I opened the door to two men in black suits. They were tall and unexpectedly handsome. Their dark beards were trimmed close to their faces. One clasped a clear plastic clipboard, and the veins on his hand bulged beautifully, as though he were lifting a barbell.

"I'm Sal," said the clipboard man, reaching his free hand toward mine to shake it. "And this is Diego."

Diego gave a polite nod and tight smile, then glanced at Sal, who offered the smallest of nods in return. At first, they had resembled twins, but now I noticed the differences between them: Diego was older, his face more creased. I felt his cool wedding band against my hand. Sal's skin was paler and his hair darker; Diego looked more Latino.

They launched into explaining the procedure, pausing every so often to ask if I had any questions. I shook my head. I'd already heard much of what they said because their spiel echoed the broadcasts on television. The procedure would be quick. It would be painless, or as painless as a regular flu shot. I wondered how many households they'd visited before mine, how many identical introductions they'd already given.

"Any questions?" Diego asked.

"I'm on my period," I blurted.

"That's fine," Sal said. "That has no bearing."

Sal unclasped his briefcase with two satisfying clicks and retrieved a set of rubber gloves. He snapped them on—they were tight on him—and rummaged for his other implements. I closed my eyes. I'm not a shot person.

I felt a hand gently brush my hair aside, away from my ears and to one side of my neck, and my eyes fluttered open for a moment, startled by the pleasantness of this contact. It was why I liked getting a haircut, that impersonal/personal touch.

"Hold still," Sal said, and I reflexively nodded. He waited for my head to finish moving. He looked at Diego with a long-suffering expression. And though I was turned away, I pictured Sal communicating back, with his look, *Just two hours to go.*

A cool alcohol swab ran over my skin, then a quick pinch, and that was all. By the time I opened my eyes, Sal was snapping his gloves off. With what seemed to me tenderness, he moved my hair back over my shoulder.

"You can go about your day as you usually would," Diego said.

"You might feel some dizziness or nausea, but that's completely normal," Sal said. "If anything worse happens, call the number on this pamphlet."

"It's a hotline," Diego added. They stood.

On the front of the pamphlet was a smiling white woman hugging a smiling white child. The pamphlet was smooth and thick—high-quality. I wondered how much it had cost the country to print pamphlets for every American. A lot. But maybe it was a better use of tax dollars than many other things tax dollars were used for.

Starting today, babies born in American hospitals would receive this injection. Regular doses of medication—for maintenance—would be put into our water supply. It would be in the tap, it would be in our bottled water. I'd heard there were critics who found the entire undertaking questionable—it was racial segregation all over again, separate but equal taken to the most extreme—but those critics grudgingly agreed to it, because what choice did we have? The violence had gotten so bad.

~~

As soon as the men left I changed back into my pajama pants. I noticed, with displeasure, that the pants were tighter. I hated shopping. I made a mental note that I would have to do something about that. Because of my mother, I'd always seen gyms as terrible places. I'd never set foot in one.

Go about your day as you usually would, the men had said. My usual days involved trading stocks and cryptocurrency, watching animal videos, and checking the messages on the online-dating services I used. My algae energy stock had gone up. My Ravencoin had gone down. A cat sat calmly on a running goat. The same four men sent me their same four penises.

Around eight p.m., I realized I hadn't eaten all day, so I decided I'd venture out for a bite. I headed to the Wendy's drive-through and ordered my regular burger.

"One Baconator," the employee repeated through the speaker. "Any fries with that?"

"No fries," I said. "Just the Baconator. And a chocolate Frosty."

"Baconator and a Frosty," she said and gave me my total.

When I pulled up to the food window, the employee who had taken my order repeated the price, and I gave her exact change. She kept her head down; her hair was pulled back and she was wearing a Wendy's visor. When she looked up to give me my burger, I noticed she was Asian. She handed me the Frosty, then passed me a straw. I put the cold cup, with its condensation beginning to bead on its sides, into my cupholder, where it balanced on some trash.

At a stoplight, I glanced down at my burger bag. Instead of the regular Wendy, with her pinkish skin, red hair, and red freckles, this Wendy's skin had a yellowish hue. Wendy's hair was black and Wendy's face was wiped clean of red freckles. Wendy, I realized, looked like me.

I pulled over at the Walmart and parked. I ate my burger quickly, then chased it with the Frosty and gave myself a brain freeze.

Inside the Walmart, I saw the cashiers were all Asian women, and all the customers were Asian women with Asian daughters in shopping carts, or Asian women maneuvering around in motorized wheelchairs. In the toy aisle, all the Barbies had black hair like mine. In the electronics section, on the TVs, all the pop singers were Asian women.

The Freshening had begun.

~~~

The fancy pamphlet had fallen between two couch cushions. I pulled it out. The smiling white woman with the smiling white child had transformed: now they were a smiling Asian woman and a smiling Asian child. I put the pamphlet face down on the coffee table.

The news was on every channel. An Asian woman reporter stood in front of a movie theater where the new summer blockbusters were playing. She stopped a bystander, an Asian woman wearing a white muscle shirt and sagging pants.

"I never thought something like this could be possible in my lifetime," the bystander said. She had gold teeth. Tears were streaming down her cheeks, and she was having difficulty speaking. The reporter patted her on the shoulder encouragingly. "I look around, and everyone is like me. Everyone's a Black man like me. Earlier today I got pulled over because one of my taillights was out. And the cop just let me go with a warning. Can you believe it?"

I opened my other bottle of wine and streamed *Mr. and Mrs. Smith*. Brad Pitt looked like Brad Pitt but he was an Asian woman, and Angelina Jolie was an Asian woman with full lips. Every supporting character and every last extra was an Asian woman.

Before I retired for the night, I looked at myself in the mirror. I was still me. I looked at the framed photo that hung above the piano: my family at my college graduation. My mother, father, and me. The photo hadn't changed, except my father was a woman. It had been taken before we found out about my father's second family, in Thailand. It had turned out they were the reason he was always "on business" there. The photo captured my mother at her happiest, in the months before we learned all this, speaking her fluent English to her American family.

When I was twenty-five, my father went to live with his other wife and other daughter.

"Good riddance" was what my mother said, not convincingly.

She sighed more than usual. I wondered if my father's other family resembled ours. His other daughter was sixteen years younger than me, and her name was Jodie.

~~

In the town where I grew up, there had been only one other Asian kid: Bruce Kim, who had the additional misfortune of being short. By kindergarten, I was better at reading and writing than all of my classmates. But the boys—and it was always the boys—made fun of me ruthlessly. They pulled the corners of their eyes up and chanted "Ching chang chong" at me, giggling.

"That doesn't mean anything," I'd mutter under my breath.

The girls were quieter, alienating me with silence rather than taunts. They never invited me to birthday parties or sleepovers.

Yet I was grateful that Bruce always got treated worse than I did. Once, he came to school with two black eyes, so that his already little eyes were almost completely disappeared in pillows of purple flesh, like two raisins in rum-raisin ice cream.

In high school, we organized ourselves by race, as though we were in prison. By then there were two other Asian girls, Kristy Tomiko and Jessica Lee. We didn't have a lot in common besides how we looked, but we had no choice but to become friends.

Our junior year, Bruce's parents found him hanging from the ceiling fan. We heard about it via an announcement over the intercom. Not the ceiling fan part, just that he had "passed." They even put it in the language of schools. Who passed, I wondered, and who failed?

When talks of the Freshening first began, my mother followed the news of it with great interest. It seemed incredibly far off as a possibility. There would be too many people to convince, too many hoops to jump through. The Freshening had been a minority woman's idea, but in order for it to be implemented nationally, the majority of Americans would have to be persuaded, and America was still a majority-white nation. Convincing them would be impossible, we thought.

My boyfriend at the time, a white man, thought it was a stupid idea. Jim not only voted against it, he protested, holding up signs that said DIVERSITY IS LIFE. Later I stumbled across a photo album he kept of former girlfriends, like an album a fisherman might keep of fish he'd caught. It was the bottommost item in a stack of things under his most intricate bong. There were ten girlfriends in all, and every last one was Asian. I was the final entry in the album. It was a photo of our trip to the Bahamas, so I was more tan than usual and wearing a tube top. There was a pale white stripe on each of my shoulders—from my spaghetti-strap bikini. I was giving a modest smile. We weren't cute together, it occurred to me all of a sudden. I'd been blind to it the whole time. I looked like a prostitute he'd picked up.

After I dumped Jim, the bill surprised us all by passing. The vast majority of white people, it turned out, wanted to go about their lives seeing only other white people. And we'd forgotten about white supremacists—there were more of them waiting quietly in the wings than we could have imagined.

"I never liked him anyway," my mother had said, about Jim.

I'd been crying into her shoulder; a perfect circle of her shirt was soaked through. It was her way of being supportive, but that didn't make it the right thing to say to your broken-up-with daughter. A white mother would have cried with me, I imagined. A white mother would have felt all the feelings I felt, in perfect empathy.

The bill passed but the medication wasn't perfect. They were working out the kinks. The government not only knew it, they readily admitted to it in the name of transparency.

We know it's not perfect yet was their disclaimer, trumpeted over and over again.

The plan was never to use us as test subjects, but then the plan became irrelevant. The riots had gotten so bad—the violence relentless. People were dropping like flies, and we were better off guinea pigs than flies.

In the beginning, everything was novel, everything was disorienting. Once we got used to things, which of course we did, problems arose.

We discriminated based on age; ageism became rampant. We discriminated based on weight—that aspect of American life hadn't changed. They decided not to freshen weight for practical reasons—that was the argument, anyway. On planes, for example.

Gangs wore clothing that showed what race they were. People impersonated other races. Babies were given ethnic names that had nothing to do with their actual ethnicity. These were growing pains, some of the pundits argued. Soon we would be postrace.

There were protests—hordes of people, Asian to me, holding up signs saying DO NOT INJECT and DIVERSITY IS BEAUTIFUL. There were counterprotests that said DIVERSITY IS GENOCIDE. Communities of nouveau race hippies lived out in the woods, having avoided the injections somehow.

~~~

As for me, I didn't join in the demonstrations. I went about my life.

I logged on to the online-dating sites that I'd used in the past. I would be lying if I didn't admit a small part of me hoped to meet someone.

In my inbox, I had a message from someone named Bill that said, I enjoyed your profile, and I, too, like Superman: The Movie. You appear to be a person of substance. Bill looked to be an Asian woman. All my prospects were Asian women. I scrutinized their profiles more carefully. The penises in my inbox were now vaginas, not dissimilar from mine.

Bill and I went to the Holocaust Museum and, afterward, to an ice-cream shop for a sundae we decided to split.

"You ladies have a nice time with that," said the employee who scooped our ice cream.

I tried to look beyond the fact that I wasn't attracted to Bill. I tried to see him for who he was on the inside, for his sense of humor and the quality of his thoughts. He attempted, I think, to do the same for me. We'd checked the box for the same political views and I found myself assuming he would agree with me on the issues of the day. When he didn't, each of us bristled. We got into an argument about whether or not Superman should have saved Lois Lane from dying in a landslide—"You don't fuck with time, even if you're Superman," Bill said, "*especially* if you're Superman"—and then an argument about Israel and Palestine. When we parted ways, it was obvious that we would not see each other again.

I joined the gym, where nobody looked at my butt. The doctor didn't assume that I was lactose intolerant, or give me a generally clean bill of health and make a joke about Asians living forever. But aside from that, nothing dramatically changed. I wasn't less alone.

About a year into the Freshening, I got together with my friend Alison, whom I knew from our lives before was mixed race and had modeled in her youth. I hadn't seen her since the change, but here we were, sitting on a park bench, eating sandwiches from a deli as though we were friends who did this sort of a thing on a regular basis. Alison told me she wanted to throw a changey party.

"But, like, classy," she said.

The underground changey parties in the newspapers were like raves from the nineties: held in warehouses, with DJs playing thumping music and everyone's clothes glowing in the dark. Sometimes the dancers overdosed and had to be rushed to the hospital. Changeys allowed you to change back—to see the world as it was for an hour or even a whole day, depending on your metabolism. When you overdosed, according to people who had come out the other side, you didn't see people at all; people resembled Picassos, like some other life-form entirely.

That was what I'd heard, anyway. I'd never had a changey myself. I didn't know the right kinds of people, or so I thought.

"Where'd you get them?" I asked.

"I have a friend. Who has a friend."

"I see."

"You never come out," she whined, as though she cared. Alison had attended my mother's funeral, and I'd appreciated that. She texted to check in once or twice in the months that followed, but then the texts stopped. I didn't blame her for this. I knew I wasn't any fun.

I still missed my mother, but lately I thought about her once a week, instead of every day—multiple times a day—like I had in the year after her death. I missed her way of acting aghast at things I said or did. I missed how she touched me on my upper arm when she wanted to reassure me. I missed her smell. There was no smell like her on Earth anymore, and there would be no way of reproducing it.

In the house we'd shared, I slept with people I met on the internet. Once or twice the sex was amazing, but mostly the sex was forgettable, even as it was happening. Nothing serious ever materialized. I told myself I didn't care, and usually I didn't. My cryptocurrency was up. I busied myself trading it.

Alison's invitation hung in the air and finally I thought, *Why not?* Alison herself had found someone new. Their name was Paul, she told me, and they had made Alison very happy. Maybe they would have friends of quality and bring them to the party. Maybe I'd meet somebody.

"I was wondering, actually," Alison added, very innocently, "if we could host it at your house? Since it's so big and everything?"

Oh, I realized.

I could count the number of times I'd thrown a party on one hand. She gave me this sweet look.

"Sure," I said, finally. "Okay."

I bought craft beers and big plastic buckets to hold them. I bought large handles of vodka and bourbon from Costco, big bottles of sodas—ginger ale, Coke, and Sprite. Then I waited.

My friend Christina arrived first. Because Christina was an Asian woman to begin with—in reality, I mean; she was Korean—she hadn't changed. She looked to me like she always did. I gestured at the offerings, feeling a little embarrassed at how full all the bottles were.

Christina poured herself a vodka soda into a large drinking glass. She appeared nervous. We made small talk about the weather. Finally, when she could bear her anxiety no longer, she asked, "Have you ever tried one of these? A changey?"

I shook my head.

"But Alison says they're totally safe," I said.

When she looked unpersuaded, I added, "Hang on." I ran upstairs, to the bathroom, and shook two multivitamins into my palm. I ran back downstairs and presented them to Christina, who gave me a small, pursed, but appreciative smile. We washed the vitamins down with vodka.

One by one the guests began to arrive. First Alison with Paul, then Alison's college roommate, Nicole, who I was disappointed to see carrying a large bottle of Coke. She handed it to me proudly and I feigned pleasure. How much Coke would I have to drink after tonight? Open Coke was such a burden. We were all still waiting for the changeys to arrive, making distracted small talk. This was, for now, just a regular old party.

I noticed Alison pacing from living room to kitchen, picking up napkins, crumpling them in her hand. "Georgina was supposed to be here, like, yesterday," she said.

"Hey, baby," Paul said. They put a hand on Alison's back, and she relaxed ever so slightly. They put their forehead against hers, and I watched them whisper something that made her relax even further. Paul was the calming force. Relationships needed that, I thought: at least one calming force. Zero calming forces was unsustainable. You could have two, but that was boring. Jim had been my calming force. But a calming force didn't count for everything. And sometimes you also needed an agitating force. I supposed that was what my mother had been. In any case, these days I had no force at all.

Christina's husband, Harry, arrived late. He'd been a rosy-complexioned redhead. We'd gone to college together, the three of us, and he had tried to date me before I introduced him to Christina. I remember the scent of his breath as he gave me a good-night kiss, like used dental floss.

Not long after they started dating, I asked if it bothered her that he had a fetish.

"No," she'd said. "I mean, I only dated white guys. How is that different?"

"It *is* different," I'd responded, without conviction.

Harry kissed me chastely on the cheek and headed to the kitchen for a beer.

Now Christina, four vodkas in, was telling me, "I miss the way he looks. And he misses the way I look."

"But don't you think it's better this way?" I asked. "Like, ultimately?"

She took a long drink.

"Maybe," she said finally, after what seemed like forever.

～

The kitchen and living room had filled with people—some I recognized and some I didn't. Some I'd known previously, but now I couldn't parse their features on an Asian face. I looked over at Alison, who was laughing at something. Georgina still hadn't arrived with the changeys. Maybe she never would. I was interested in experiencing the drugs, of course, but there was a part of me that hoped she would never arrive. The way, when you're losing your virginity, you hope the other person will change their mind so you don't have to actually go through with it.

When Georgina stepped into the room, we almost didn't notice. But of course we noticed, because she was Georgina. Georgina had an Afro and beautiful features, set into any race of face.

"Hey bitches," she said, cheerfully. By now most of us were pretty drunk. It was past eleven.

Alison made a beeline for her.

"Do you have them?" she slurred. Her eyes were huge and eager. I was reminded of why I didn't like spending time with Alison—because she always wanted something from you.

"I do," Georgina said. "Plenty for everybody. Hey, can I get a drink or something first?" She laughed, in the way truly confident people laugh.

I fetched her a rum and Coke, which I remembered was her drink. She gazed at me—with a look of pity, I thought; I was too eager, too openly pathetic—then thanked me.

Georgina reached into her purse and retrieved two pill bottles.

We all watched silently as she shook them into Alison's open palm. They spilled out with a sound like Scrabble tiles and were beautiful—pearly green, the size of Tic Tacs.

～

Alison placed a single precious changey into each of our open palms. I caught Christina's eye from across the crowded room. It was a relief to know that whatever happened, she'd stay the same; we'd stay the same to each other.

Everyone's heads tilted back, swallowing their changeys in a synchronized dance. I swallowed my changey a moment after everyone else. The pill left a little emerald stain where it had sat on my sweating hand. We made awkward small talk while we waited for the effects to settle in. The small talk was even more strained than normal. It was as though we had suddenly sobered with the realization of what was about to happen.

～

I heard the changeys beginning to work before I saw the changes for myself.

"Shit," Alison said. I saw her looking at Paul, who wore a guilty look, as though they'd been caught stealing.

"I'm sorry, baby, I'm sorry," Paul pleaded.

My changey still wasn't working. I wondered if it was a dud. To me, Alison and Paul were still two Asian women who didn't look happy, whose relationship, I knew, would not endure this night.

~~~

Upstairs, people were arguing, people were ripping clothes off one another's diverse bodies. The sound was deafening. It would have been a matter of time before my neighbors complained, but they weren't complaining because many were here, too—I'd invited them. All night Maxine, my across-the-street neighbor, had been leaning against my mother's credenza, talking to Joey, my down-the-street neighbor. Now I knew their changeys were taking hold, because I watched Maxine's body stiffen and their conversation—whose natural progression was to get easier—grow more stilted. I watched Joey, responding to Maxine, stiffen, too.

I opened the door to the guest room, where I found Christina making out with someone who didn't look to be Harry. I'd recently gone through a phase of preparing for the apocalypse. Now plastic bins filled the room. It had started with a knapsack of tampons and menstrual pads, for the obvious reasons, but also because I'd read tampons could be useful for any bleeding. Tampons might replace currency, according to the internet, so I bought thousands. I'd stockpiled this room with gallons of water, emergency blankets, flares. Though I was failing in this world, I held out hope that, sufficiently prepared, I could do better in the next. The person had pinned Christina against a plastic bin filled with tampons.

The person's breathing was loud and labored and masculine. He burrowed his head passionately between her breasts, like a gopher boring through packed dirt. I shut the door.

I remembered I'd had the foresight to lock my bedroom. I let myself in and deadbolted the door behind me, like I was in a zombie movie. The zombies were my friends, but what could I do? They'd changed. The relief was immediate.

I sat on the floor at the foot of the queen bed. I closed my eyes, tried not to listen to the particular words that were being spoken throughout the house—words of shock, horror, disbelief, anger, grief, passion, lust. In the fairy tales my mother read to me as a child, blond children populated the pages, and for years I never realized the difference between them and me, until one day I did. After that, I never felt like a princess. Even now, every night on my expensive queen mattress, I felt like the pea.

I took the ancient VCR from my closet. I plugged its cords into the television set. I had only four VHS tapes in my possession, and those, of course, were *Superman*s one through four. I wiped off the VCR's dusty mouth with my sleeve and inserted *Superman*.

I knew the movie by heart. My changey was definitely a dud—it couldn't be taking this long—and this was just my luck. Christopher Reeve was an Asian woman and Margot Kidder was an Asian woman. I mouthed the words along with the actors.

When I closed my eyes, I could picture the scene that was to come: Christopher Reeve flying around the Earth to rotate it backward, to save Lois. He'd bring my mother back to life, to bring us back to a time before all this. I tried to remember Christopher Reeve's actual face, not the Asian face I saw. Was that a better time? Maybe it wasn't, and yet, I'll be honest, I still longed for it.

When I opened my eyes, Christopher Reeve wasn't an Asian woman any longer. He had become Christopher Reeve again, with his beautifully blue eyes and very plasticky-looking black hair—a helmet with a single stiff curl. He was screaming because Margot Kidder was lying on the ground beside her car, dead.

Downstairs, people were also screaming. Not in a sad, mournful way, but in an angry, deafening way. There was the sound of dishes or glasses or windows breaking, then of sirens—first distant, then incredibly close. Someone had called the police, or an ambulance—maybe someone was hurt. Though it was my house—my mother's house—I didn't want to go downstairs. Later, I thought. Not yet.

In the movie, Superman flew furiously around the Earth. He flew and flew and there was thunder and various special effects that seemed, admittedly, lame now. When he flew back to Margot Kidder, he found her alive—she was in her car trying to start it. Her light brown eyes, wide open, took him in. It had worked. He'd turned back time. Christopher Reeve didn't let on that he had done anything, and I loved that. If I were Margot Kidder, I wouldn't have wanted to know, either. It would have been terrible, to feel, for the rest of your life, in permanent debt.

Someone banged loudly on my door and shouted my name. I didn't respond; I stayed incredibly quiet. I lived here, but that was all. What could I do? The damage was already done.

SLOW AND STEADY

It was too late for us to get drunk and fall into bed together. Not too late in the day—it was nine a.m. I mean too late in life. Our timing was off. It had started being off before we had ever met, which was at age eighteen, in the library of our Ivy League university, where we both had jobs reshelving books. He left me notes in the stacks and I left him notes by the water fountain—not notes, exactly, but call numbers—tip-offs to good book titles. We'd both wanted to be writers. It was never romantic between us, but it wasn't not flirting.

We were thirty-five now. I was in Los Angeles for a meeting, and we were in the same popular café. I had been eyeing the pastries, not wanting one exactly. He'd gotten close in order to confirm it was me, and I hadn't noticed—so intently was I considering a bear claw.

"Sophie," he said, his face breaking into a smile. "Long time."

"Gabe," I said, shocked. It had been. It had been thirteen years, and he wasn't on Instagram, meaning I didn't know more about him than I should have. In fact, I knew next to nothing. His hair was less long and less unruly than it had been in college. I'd always found him beautiful, I suddenly remembered, with a clarity that took me by surprise.

"What are you getting?" He turned to me, at the cash register.

"Just . . . a coffee, I guess."

"Regular coffee?"

The barista looked at him, eyebrow lifting. All these questions, while the line ballooned.

"Yeah," I said, glancing behind us, flustered.

"I was, too. Should we just get one big one? And share it? We'd save"—a pause while he did a silent calculation—"one dollar and twenty-two cents."

The proposition seemed bold—intimate, even—but I found myself saying, "Sure. Okay."

"One big coffee," the barista repeated.

"And a bear claw," Gabe added. In fluid movements, he passed the parceled pastry off to me, while he sipped a bit of liquid from the full cup and brought it, without spilling, to the station with the milk and the sugar. He pointed at both: Did I want them? I nodded. With a long-handled metal spoon he mixed in the sugar. The crystals were big and light brown. He sipped, then handed it to me to try. It was perfect.

"Hi, by the way," he said, and leaned in for a hug.

As I pulled away, I held my breath, out of habit. He still made me nervous. In college, kids like him had frightened me—kids with parents who had taken them to museums as children, who had been raised to express their opinions at the dinner table. My immigrant parents had taken me to libraries, so I wasn't totally hopeless. Books had taught me some things, though not all.

I'd never been Gabe's type, and I knew it. He'd dated rich

girls with clear blue eyes and long soft hair, who came from families with vacation homes. At our college, it was rich people and white people and rich white people who boldly embarked on sexual encounters and long vacations, and proclaimed opinions in our philosophy seminars. I'd gotten over this, I'd thought. And yet here I was, with my heart beating faster than usual.

I thought about all of this as we stood together, taking turns sipping coffee.

"Where are you headed?" he asked.

"Honestly?" I said. "Nowhere." I held up my folded newspaper as proof. "I was planning on doing the crossword."

"Coincidence," he said. "Me, too."

I must have looked hesitant, because he added, "Are you anti-collaboration?"

I laughed. "No, no. Pro-collaboration. I welcome your assistance."

We sat at one of the tables outside, beneath a trellis—wisteria hanging down. Around us, there were flowers and cacti and weeds that looked thrown there, but perfect in that rambling, Los Angeles way. Sunlight dappled the crossword. How strange it was that we were both here, I thought. I'd flown in from Chicago only yesterday.

After working our way through half the crossword with ease, we stalled. He moved my hand gently because it was covering a clue; he touched my wedding ring as he did.

"Eight down," he read aloud. "Slow and steady."

"No idea." I shook my head.

For a long moment, we sat in silence.

"Why don't we go?" he said. "Walking could shake something up. Slow and steady."

"Sure," I said, picking up my purse.

As we walked, we talked. We'd wanted to be writers and now we were. He told me about writing for a popular television show, and I told him the plot of my third novel. He showed me a picture of his dog, and I pulled up a picture of mine. To find the photo I had to scroll past photos of my own family. I found myself not wanting to share those. An hour passed like this, walking and talking, and I didn't know where we were any longer.

As we walked past men in orange breaking apart the sidewalk, one of them jackhammering, Gabe said something, but I couldn't hear it.

"What?" I shouted.

"I said you're the same," he said, too loud, because by the next block it was quiet: bird chirps and distant airplanes overhead. I thought of the phrase *noise pollution*. Was every noise pollution? Or was it a certain amount of noise, all collected, at a high volume, that made it qualify as pollution? I thought of everything we'd said to each other today, and how it was already dissipating, how it would eventually fade into nothing.

Though he'd said it admiringly, I hoped it wasn't true—that I was the same. I hoped I was different. I said, "You, too," and I meant this.

I'd envied him then, and now, this coherence—that his inner and outer natures were aligned. My fear got in the way of communicating exactly who I was; what I wanted to say always came out wrong. It was why I was a writer—so I could carefully consider and say what I meant.

I would have liked to think I'd caught up to him. I had gained some confidence, or learned to project it. I went on book tours and read aloud and more or less said what I thought. Around him I still stuttered.

"Are you married?" I blurted.

"No," he said. "But look." He stopped walking, reached into his pants pocket, pulled out a small velvet pouch. We were paused beside a tall cactus with arms that flexed up. He shook the ring out into my hand, and it made a pleasing clinking noise against my own ring.

"It's beautiful." I meant it.

"My girlfriend's in the park, actually," he said, gesturing. "With the dog. Want to meet them? My family?" I could tell he was trying that word out, liking it. I wondered what my own was up to in this moment.

We were at the park's edge. From our distance, we could see her: she was sitting on a bench, peering into her phone, and the green grass all around her was dotted with dandelions, yellow and white, young and old. I saw her long blond hair with a baseball cap over it and knew that must be her. She flicked a tennis ball to a border collie that ran to fetch it. I felt a swell of something, like loss. Also betrayal: I thought we'd been wandering, but now I realized he had led me, purposely, here.

"Is she an actress?" My voice came out cracked, soft.

"She went to school for nursing. But yeah, you know. This city. She acts now."

I realized, suddenly, that he was being modest. I had seen her movies before. She was actually very famous. I realized I knew things about her love life because I had read about it in magazines at the dentist's office. Gabe had been left largely out of the tabloids, but I knew that before him, she'd dated an actor who played the main superhero in a superhero movie. That she was now dating Gabe didn't come as a surprise. He wasn't famous or even particularly striking, but it didn't matter. He was intelligent and a lively conversationalist, and because he exuded his strange confidence, he'd always dated the most beautiful women.

"What's your dog's name?"

"He's Harry. He's a sweetheart. And smart."

As he started to walk toward her and I trailed behind, I said, "No, wait."

I wanted to get close enough to smell the perfume she wore at the same time that I really, really didn't.

He looked at me, curious.

"I think I should head back."

"What? Really?"

"Yeah. I'm sorry." I turned my wrist, but I wasn't wearing my watch. I'd forgotten it. "I should go."

"I'm so sorry," I added. "Next time." I cringed at this. I didn't mean it. I was saying things just to say them.

We'd long since tossed our shared coffee cup and our hands were empty. He took both of mine in his. My hands were cold in his warm ones.

"Well, it was good to see you, Sophie. Running into you, it makes me . . ." He trailed off. "It's good to see you," he repeated. "We could see each other on purpose sometime. Let me know when you're in LA again."

"I'd like that," I said.

Back at my hotel room I stripped naked, and put on the too long and too thick terry bathrobe. I had a missed call from my husband. He'd called the hotel, and so the black plastic phone blinked red with its voice message. We made it a point to call each other's hotels whenever one of us was away. It felt more special to receive a message tied to a physical place.

"We miss you," he said. *We* meant him and our toddler and our dog, my family. "It's raining here. I found your note."

I'd left him a note inside his pillow, not expecting him to

notice it overnight, and I was right. I would have noticed the crispy paper right away, but he didn't, and it was one of the things I loved about him. "And I figured out what 'slow and steady' was, in case you're stuck on it. I don't think it counts as cheating."

The phone stopped blinking, once the message had been heard. I went to the bathroom, where I peered into the little round mirror, the one that enlarged everything disgusting on my face: my broken capillaries and dull skin and giant pores, the lines around my eyes and my black hair that was split at the ends. I wondered if this was what actresses also saw in those round mirrors, or if they looked into them and were pleased.

Gabe and I had kissed in college, just once. All day, I'd held the memory at bay. In thirteen years, I hadn't let myself recall it. Now I wondered if it could really have been me who lived it.

It was senior year and we were at an off-campus party. We'd tried spin the bottle with an empty wine bottle, and it was more boring than we anticipated, kissing people so openly and so lightly, so we'd moved on. What about Seven Minutes in Heaven? someone joked. We wrote our names on scraps of paper and threw them into a salad bowl. I watched Gabe as he dropped his hand into the bowl and drew out a slip of paper and read it aloud: "Sophie." What were the ridiculous odds? I'd been terrified it wouldn't be me and now was terrified that it was. Lila and Daniel were in the closet, and Billy had tasked himself with timing them. He banged on the door when the seven minutes were up, and my heart stopped. We were next.

The closet was pitch-black except for the strip of light at the bottom. I had been drinking all night but suddenly felt extraordinarily, terrifically sober. "Since you picked me," I said, "does that mean you get to do whatever you want?" It was suddenly very difficult to breathe, less oxygen in a closet, I supposed, and I wondered if my breath seemed labored. I tried to adjust it; I didn't want to seem like I was making too big a deal out of this. But I hadn't done this before, not even in middle school—especially not in middle school.

"We don't have to do anything if you don't want to," Gabe said kindly. We were pressed up together in the small closet, and all the coats smelled like a thrift store. I wondered if he could hear how fast my heart was beating.

"We could just—" He swished some of the clothes around, to make it seem like something exciting was happening.

I put my hand against his face and reached my fingers up to some of the hair that spilled out from behind his ears. He took that for the invitation that it was. He leaned in to kiss me so softly that I hardly registered it was happening. I thought everyone had been drinking the same disgusting vodka concoction, but his mouth tasted like Sprite—was that all he'd had?—and my whole body thrummed, wanting more, knowing that whatever we wound up doing would not be enough in the slightest. Emboldened, I kissed him back, and he pushed me against some synthetic fur, and an ironing board fell over from where it was propped on top of us. We were in college; who ironed? We repositioned ourselves and resumed. I tried not to think of how Gabe had probably touched a thousand girls in this same way. I tried not to think about how we would never speak of this again. I wondered how many minutes had passed. It was too many minutes, whatever it was.

When our seven minutes were up, Billy knocked on the door. He opened it with a disgusting, pimp-like grin. We spilled out into the light. I smoothed my hair and Gabe smoothed his and we looked around. Nobody was there but Billy. Everyone had lost interest in the game. The closet door stayed open.

"Can I get you a beer?" Gabe had said then. Casually, as though we hadn't just had our tongues in each other's mouths.

"Sure," I said. We trudged silently to the keg, trying to appear normal. Gabe pumped the keg expertly, handed me my cup. He watched me sip from it.

"You don't want one?" I asked.

"I have a test in the morning," he said. "Unfortunately."

He touched my shoulder. I couldn't meet his eye. This had been a game to him, I suddenly realized. It was a game, of course. I had been seven of a million minutes he'd had in heaven, and I felt ashamed, as I always did, and as I would for years to come—not about this forgotten thing specifically, but ashamed, more generally, that things were a bigger deal to me than they were to other people. I'd worked hard to cultivate the opposite—to care less—and, mostly, I'd succeeded.

"Hey, this is for you," Gabe said, and handed me a small folded note that looked like the kind he'd leave for me to find in the stacks at the library. "Don't open it till I'm gone, okay?" he added.

I nodded. Obediently, I put it in my pocket. After Gabe left, I finished my beer, alone. There was no one I cared to talk to. I perched the cup on top of the overflowing trash bin and walked back to my dorm room, my body humming more loudly with the embarrassment and longing I felt constantly, like a broken machine. The longing was to be someone different, someone better.

~~~

I'd already changed into pajamas and climbed into bed when I remembered the note in my pocket; I removed it from my jeans. I wondered if it was one of our call numbers—something funny for me to look up in the library later. Neither of us worked there anymore. I'd gotten a different job, and Gabe had never needed, financially, to work there to begin with. I unfolded it. Instead of the familiar series of numbers and letters it said only a name. The slip of paper read "Nadia," but he had lied, and announced it was me. I remembered that now. The rest was a blur.

TAPETUM LUCIDUM

There were two other Asian woman–white man couples at the animal shelter—two in addition to Sam and me, that is. They stood at the same windows, peering at the same dogs, pressing their fingers to the glass. They spent time in the kitten rooms like we had. I wondered if the kittens could tell the difference—preferred some of us over the others, had a sense of who could give them better qualities of life, who was purer of heart. I wondered if they acted adorable, accordingly.

In one room, a sleek, short-haired, muscular dog had produced three puddles of completely liquid poo. He stepped around them to approach the window, through which he looked at us, eyes shimmering with guilt. The sign on his window said his name was Max, and that he was three years old. Max had likely done something that had gotten him ejected from his previous home. Most dogs were in rooms with one or two other dogs, but Max was alone in his enclosure. This was a telling detail, too.

There was a chute into which you could drop a treat so I slid Max one, then two more, feeling sorry for him. It occurred to me the treats might have caused the liquid poo, and I instantly regretted it. But he appeared so happy to be eating them. He left wet spots where his mouth met the floor.

Until this point, we had thought of ourselves as dog people. We enjoyed nature and long walks. I wasn't athletic, in particular, but I could throw a Frisbee and Sam had played Ultimate. Frisbees were dog items. Cat people were poorly socialized, we'd been led to believe, whereas we were well-adjusted and outdoorsy. But at the kitten window, one kitten gave us pause. The kitten seemed especially awkward among its peers. It had a white coat with random patches of brown and black: the same coloring as one of those lucky Japanese cats, with the paw that goes up and down. We watched it bat around a faux mouse, alone, unable to join the free-spirited play of its roommates, who were all the same gray color, and seemed like brothers.

The shelter volunteers wore vests and black shirts on which you could see copious amounts of affixed animal hair. It wasn't exactly an advertisement for having a pet. All the volunteers carried hand sanitizer and squeezed clear dimes into their palms at every opportunity. The woman who opened the door to the kitten room had a thick coating of yellow plaque on her teeth.

The kitten was a she. The kitten's name—the name that the shelter had given her—was Sheila. Like a human baby, Sheila was helplessly floppy. Her head lolled against Sam's chest. When Sam brought her close to his face she looked curiously into his eyes, fogging up his glasses with her breath, making a tiny, perfect fog circle.

"We should think about it," I said, out of habit, though the decision seemed already made.

Sam handed Sheila back to the volunteer, who returned her to her enclosure.

We had been trying to conceive a child—or at least, not trying to prevent a child—but getting a pet we hadn't discussed or even considered.

We glanced into the window again. While the other cats were playing, our kitten hung off one of the perches, eyes closed and making a kneading motion in the air, following her own bliss.

"She's making biscuits," said the shelter volunteer.

"Let's walk around the block," Sam suggested.

In silence, we left the building.

"How long do cats live for?" I asked.

He took out his phone, typed out the question.

"Fifteen to twenty years," he read.

"Whoa."

"It's a long time," he agreed.

We both said nothing, doing quiet calculations. If the cat lived to twenty, I would be fifty-five when she died. We'd each made this same quiet calculation when we decided to get married last year except that, to marriage, there would be no end.

Sam never asked me to marry him in the grand way that happens on TV. He had pitched it, one night, like a dinner restaurant we should try.

"Sure," I'd said, as casually.

At City Hall, there had been couples of all stripes: old, young, young and old, gay, straight, interracial, intraracial. It had felt like a joyful DMV. Getting married at least gave us some gravitas. At least marriage suggested you weren't dabbling.

Outside, couples were struggling to walk the dogs they were considering taking home. There was another interracial couple, trying out a pit bull. The man was Indian or Pakistani, and he was holding a taut leash—the pit bull at the other end of it lunged desperately forward, as if toward freedom. The man's biceps were chiseled, accentuated from effort. The dog's teeth were bared, and its gums were creepy—splotched with black and pink, like they'd been spray-painted with a malfunctioning can. The woman was white and walked alongside them. On occasion, she reached out to tentatively pat the pit bull's head. Would they take this animal home? It seemed ill-advised. Was what we were doing ill-advised, too? I wondered if we should get an outside opinion, but there was no one to ask—not my family, especially.

"Let's do it," Sam said, at last. It was what I had been thinking, too.

It was strange that we were now so willing to make these big decisions, when I still struggled, at drugstores, to commit to a brand of toothpaste. I wondered what made these weighty decisions suddenly possible, after all the time in which they had not been possible.

～～

The box to transport the kitten home was made from sturdy cardboard and had holes punched into it. We had been handed the box by a shelter volunteer, but couldn't see into it. We could only make out a pair of glowing eyes. We joked that they had given our chosen pet away to another Asian–white person couple, mistaking them for us.

At home, we opened the box, prepared for the worst. We would keep whatever cat it was. This was the sort of people we prided ourselves in being: true to our word. It turned out to be the correct cat. Sheila jumped out of the box in one easy, elegant motion. After exploring the bathroom, she investigated the rest of our small apartment. Most fascinating to her was a rubber band she found beneath the fridge.

Sheila did many things silently. She even walked silently. We seemed vulgar by comparison. One moment she was there and then she wasn't. One moment she was in a paper bag and the next, she was inside the underwear drawer, asleep.

When we called Sam's parents to tell them that we'd gotten a cat, Sam's mother said to us, "How wonderful!"

"I expect lots of photos," she added, and we laughed.

"I'm way ahead of you," I said to my mother-in-law.

When I told my parents, my mother asked, "Why did you get a cat? Don't you want to travel?"

My father joked about it getting killed within the year—hit by a car.

"She's an indoor cat," I clarified.

I expected this of them. It was the difference between my Chinese parents and Sam's white ones. These days we called one set of parents and then the other, and instead of the juxtaposition making me disappointed, like it used to, it now amused me. My parents loved me. They would take bullets for me. But they were as uninterested in Sheila as they were in my emotional life. Though I tried very hard not to let it, this reality still occasionally saddened me.

"You can't have a cat and a baby," said my sister.

She had come over to meet the cat. She looked unmoved while Sheila adorably swatted at a ribbon I'd tied to a chair. My sister would, from time to time, reach out to give Sheila a tentative pat.

My sister's favorite thing to do in life was pronounce things about mine. She knew exactly how I should live. The answer was: like her.

"It's bad for the baby," she said.

I had gotten my IUD removed and now we were waiting to see if a baby would materialize. We hoped it would at the same time we hoped it wouldn't, and I'd told her as much.

"I'll research it," I said, so she would drop it.

My sister was a gynecologist. She was married to a Chinese man. She had two Chinese children, who had been very cute Chinese babies. All these decisions had thrilled my parents. Despite the fact that she was sometimes a know-it-all, and sometimes a pain in the ass, I was grateful to her for alleviating some of the pressure on me. I'd gone to a liberal arts college, studied a useless subject, and was married to a white man to whom they were polite but didn't feel at ease with. Instead of answering their questions about children, I'd now gotten a pet.

My sister had had a pet once—her family had. George had been her children's short-lived hamster. The children had set George free, in a spirit of generosity, and he'd gotten promptly run over by a bread truck. It was a harsh sequence of events—some real-life shit in the span of minutes.

There had been a debate about whether or not to collect George, whose body was completely unrecognizable, and to give him a proper burial. My sister was the one who had to scrape him off the street with a spatula. Of course it had fallen to her. She was the family's toughest cookie. I'd always been a soft thing, falling apart, like oatmeal raisin. She was a digestif cracker. While the others wept, she put George into a paper cup and dutifully dug the hole. I thought I noticed a tear in the corner of her eye but never got close enough to confirm it.

I'd never seen my sister cry. I felt close to her, but we rarely talked about anything particularly intimate. When I finally mustered the courage to tell her I was dating Sam, she said, "Okay." When I showed her a photo of him on my phone, she said, "Okay," again, and nothing more. This was my family.

~~~

Every morning I made myself coffee and Sam, who had anxiety, made himself tea. Before he left for the clinic he fed Sheila dry kibble, which made a satisfying rattling sound when we put it in her bowl, and which she crunched on, *crunch crunch crunch*. One morning, a few coffee beans slipped onto the floor and Sheila didn't hesitate to eat them up. Five minutes later, caffeine high, she zoomed around the apartment like a blind bird, knocking into things and scaring herself with the loud sounds of them falling over. There was a wild look in her eyes, and I instinctively placed my hand over my neck. Was she ever tempted to slash my throat open with her sharp claws?

People kept telling me that if you died at home a dog would wait a few days before eating you, but a cat would eat you right away. It would start with your eyes. They said this to me like I should mind it, but I didn't, as a person who values practicality. Everyone acted like it was a contest: Which animal was more depraved? I'd also heard that in a household with both dogs and cats, a dog would root around in the cat's litter box, excavate, and eat the cat's poo. A dog would dig your menstrual pad out of the trash. So how was that any better? Animals were, across the board, disgusting.

Every night, when we were in bed, the cat gazed at me intently, and I would make a big show of breathing, so she wouldn't go straight for my eyes.

One night, I had a hand on Sheila's small body, and it felt like it wasn't moving, that she wasn't breathing, that she was slightly colder than she normally was. My heart beat wildly; I started to panic. I slid her body closer to mine. It felt limp and I almost screamed in fear. But then she stirred, and gave me a face that said, *What?*

I collected her closer.

Sam was next to us, his body breathing theatrically—obscenely. With a smaller body, death seemed more plausible, that its mechanisms might just suddenly fail. With a larger one, death was more abstract. It seemed impossible that one day his could stop breathing, could cease being a source of warmth.

Was love essentially the feeling you didn't want another creature to die? There was more to it, certainly, but that had to be a biggie. I reached out to hold Sam's hand—our left hands, where our wedding rings would have been. We didn't wear rings. I wouldn't have minded one, but it wasn't Sam's style.

"Do you have rings?" the judge who married us had asked, at City Hall.

"No," we'd said, in unison.

"Okay," she'd said, unsurprised.

She must have been in her mid-seventies. I was sure she was used to seeing everything—abundant interracial couples, every sort of combo. No rings was the least of it.

～

A veterinary checkup was recommended at six months, so I made an appointment at a practice rated highly on Yelp.

In the main waiting area there were dogs of all sizes. Sheila, from inside her carrier, hissed at each of them. We moved to the sequestered cat lounge, where there was a basket of fleece blankets for throwing over cats' carriers. The receptionist poked her head into the room.

"Sheila?" she called.

I raised my hand and carried Sheila over to the examination room. A nurse greeted us. She arranged a line of treats on the table and pushed her thermometer into the cat's butt. The thermometer read 102 degrees, a normal cat temperature. She left us to wait for the doctor.

The vet came in, holding a clipboard, very much resembling a vet in his white coat. I was surprised to see that he was handsome. He was only a little taller than I was, and he looked my age. He was Vietnamese, I assumed from his last name. A Vietnamese vet. He smiled when he saw the two of us—me with a hand on the cat's wetted back.

"I see she found the automatic faucet," he said.

"She did."

"Hello," he said to the cat. He didn't use a baby voice like everyone else did with kittens. Despite the lack of that voice, which I uniformly used with her, she still recognized that he was speaking to her. She gave a bold meow.

"I'm actually wondering," I said, "if I could have her tested for toxoplasmosis."

After the conversation with my sister, I'd looked up pregnancy and cats. Websites warned about toxoplasmosis, which was caused by a single-celled parasite called *Toxoplasma gondii*, which could be in a cat's feces. Toxoplasmosis could cause birth defects in an unborn child. It could mess up a baby's vision. This bacteria impressed me. It was impressively pernicious. It lived in mice, but could sexually reproduce only in cats' guts, so what it did was change its host mouse's brain, making it unafraid of cats. The changed, bolder mouse would get eaten, and the parasite would complete its life cycle.

"We can do that," the vet said, stroking the cat's back. She purred contentedly at his touch.

"I'm thinking of getting pregnant," I added quickly. At this, I felt myself redden.

"You should know," he said, "that it's not a big deal if she tests positive. Do you have someone who could take over the litter box responsibilities?"

Was I alone? he seemed to be asking. Or if I was partnered, was my partner the sort of person who would take over a chore for me?

"I do," I said. Willing myself to stop only made me blush more deeply.

The cat was pacing the counter and the vet placed a pen in front of her, enticing her to play. She swatted at it.

"You're a beautiful cat," he said to her, in his gentle way that wasn't babying or patronizing. "I don't say it to every cat." He laughed, reading my mind.

After that, I found myself saying things in order to try to get him to smile, because I loved his smile. It produced these dimples. They weren't perfectly symmetrical; one was deeper than the other.

"She looks very healthy," he said, "but for the toxoplasmosis test we'll take her to the back to draw some blood. You can wait in the lobby."

"Okay."

"Here's my card," he added.

I noticed he didn't wear a wedding ring. His eyes fell toward my hand, maybe to see if I was wearing one.

I returned to the cat lounge to wait. The nurse approached, quiet and feline. Inside her carrier, Sheila wore a stunned expression, as though she wasn't sure what had just happened. I was disappointed that it was the nurse handing me the cat carrier rather than the vet. The receptionist told me that they would call me with the test results and I wondered who would be doing the calling. My heart pounded wildly, as though it filled my whole body. I threw his card away.

~~~

It was the handsome vet who called to tell me that the cat did not have toxoplasmosis. Which meant I was fine to clean the litter box, though I should probably still wear gloves to be on the safe side. You could never be too safe, was what everyone seemed to think about pregnancy.

Sam was at work, as he was every weekday. As an ophthalmologist, he made four times what I did. I worked freelance, which meant I was mostly home. In the beginning, when we'd first started dating, I would call him at work, with no particular agenda, just wanting to say hello. Eventually, hearing the practiced patience in his responses to my questions, I realized that the calls exasperated him. He found it hard to switch gears: from macular degeneration and myopia to whatever inanity I was calling about. I learned to save my conversation for when he was home.

―

The vet had a beautiful voice. I started to imagine his mouth on mine and stopped, reminding myself not to go there.

"Everything okay? Any questions?"

"Yes," I said. "I mean yes, I'm okay," I corrected. "No questions."

Don't go there, I thought. *Don't go there.*

Instead of going there, I picked up my phone. I opened Instagram to see if my ex-boyfriend's wife had posted photos of their children. It seemed they'd produced a new baby. Though this ex and I had been terrible for each other, there was a small part of me that still thought very fondly of him and wanted him to be okay. I wondered if he was still bad in bed, or if his wife had decided to say something to him about it. Their babies were white. If we'd stayed together, we would have had half-Chinese babies. I wondered where we would have lived, and if I would be doing something other than freelance photography, and if he would have proposed to me with a ring. I supposed the probability was yes, to all those questions. In photos, both he and his wife wore rings. He had always wanted to get married, even when we were young and it made no sense. He'd guided his life in exactly the way he wanted, at least this aspect of it.

~~

No toxoplasmosis, I texted to Sam. Texts were okay. Let's have a baby.

No prob, he texted back, with the emoji wearing nerd glasses.

What I loved most about Sam was his patience—his extraordinary capacity to wait. We'd known each other in college, when he'd been my ex's roommate. He'd seen the two of us go through a horrible breakup and reconciliation, over and over. He'd given me glasses of water when I showed up drunk and crying at their dorm room, when the ex was out with someone else. Senior year, when I'd been stranded at our East Coast school before Thanksgiving—I had intended to go to my ex's; he had broken up with me again—Sam invited me home to Rhode Island. We drove the four hours there, having a good time. And when the ex called me the night *before* Thanksgiving, Sam took me to his house in Hartford. It had all been ridiculous. Sometimes I couldn't believe Sam had known me back then—the mess I was—and still wanted to be with me now.

~~

I'd done wedding photography in the recent past. Now I photographed homes for real estate agencies and vacation rental listings. It was less fraught—unlike brides, houses weren't self-conscious or demanding. It was why I'd made the switch. But it was boring, if I was being honest.

Meanwhile, Sheila grew. In no time at all she was an adolescent cat.

"Expect decreased affection," I read online.

Her strangest new behavior was that she was easily spooked. She made a posture like a Halloween cat—arched back and ears flattened against her head. She made strange sounds and sometimes she ran beneath the bed to hide, for no apparent reason.

"There's nothing there, Sheila," I'd say, in my most soothing voice. I'd lift up the bed skirt to see her suspicious, glowing eyes.

The reason cats look like demons at night is that they have a layer to their eyes called the tapetum lucidum, I read. Other animals, with the exception of primates and humans, have it, too. Cows have it and dogs have it. In Latin it means "shining layer." The layer reflects light. What primates and humans lack in this extra layer we make up for in perception.

I followed her to see what was scaring her: Was it a moth? A shadow? A swirl of dust? I could never tell. Sheila's pupils narrowed and widened suspiciously. My perception was lacking.

Can cats see ghosts? I typed into the search engine. Online, there was no shortage of opinions.

~~~

The vet's number was still in my phone under "Recent Calls," though not saved as a contact.

"I think she might have fleas," I told him.

"Bring her over," he said. "Let's check it out."

In the exam room, he ran his slender fingers over her fur.

"I don't see them," he said.

"Well," I said, "I'm actually not sure. Either they're fleas or they're bedbugs. I have these bites."

"May I see them?" the vet asked, gently.

"Yes," I whispered.

I lifted my shirt to let him see the small raised bumps on my arms and torso. The cat watched with her head tilted.

"Fleas," he confirmed.

He wrote the name of the medication down on a scrap of paper and told me to look for it online.

"You don't even need a prescription. It's topical." He picked up Sheila and pointed to the space between her shoulder blades. "Right here," he said. "So she can't get to it when she's grooming herself."

The Vietnamese veterinarian's kiss caught me off guard—honest. His face was smooth, unlike Sam's. It was more angular. It was cooler in temperature. It shocked me.

"I'm married," I blurted, when we pulled apart. "I just don't have a ring."

I hadn't truly meant to flirt, except that I had. I'd guided his fingers to my ribs.

"I'm sorry," he said. "I read that wrong."

You read it right, I thought, but didn't say. Sheila and I went home and I antagonized her, so she would scratch me, so I would be punished for what I'd done.

~~~

While Sam was at work, I cleaned the litter box wearing gloves. A month passed, then two, then three, and I still wasn't pregnant. Sheila reached sexual maturity, capable of being impregnated, if not for the fact that she'd been spayed when we got her. So it was sort of a nothing milestone. I, on the other hand, was beginning to wonder if I'd missed my window of childbearing. We would see. *Time flies like an arrow,* I thought. *Fruit flies like a banana.* I imagined bananas overhead, winged and soaring. We tried to have a baby and we tried to have a baby and when my parents and sister and friends asked I pretended I didn't want one.

Though she was officially an adult cat, out of her adolescence, Sheila still acted strange. She flattened her ears and arched her back. Her pupils were big black holes. I spoke to her in gentle tones so she would remember that I was her provider and protector, yet she still seemed unnerved on a daily basis.

~~~

One morning, after Sam had left for work, wandering the house in search of chores to do, I followed Sheila into the kitchen. I gasped. I dropped my mug of coffee and it broke, spilling coffee everywhere. The handsome vet was there, in our kitchen. Had he gotten our address from my paperwork? Even then, how had he gotten inside? He was at the stove, as though cooking something, with his back turned to us.

"Hi," I said, but he didn't respond. I repeated myself. Again, he didn't register it. It was as though he couldn't hear me.

He walked around the kitchen with confidence, as though he'd been here before—as though he'd designed it himself. He stepped around the spilled coffee. He knew which cabinet doors to open to find a pan, to collect a plate and silverware. He made himself an omelet. Sheila and I watched his movements. He could see her, and she could see him. Sometimes he reached down to pet her and she would purr, happily.

I called my mom.

"What's wrong?" she said instead of hello.

"Do we have a history of mental illness in our family?" I asked.

"What?"

"Does anyone see things that aren't there?"

"Of course not," my mom said. "Don't be crazy."

I wondered if she would tell me if we actually did. This was another thing my parents might not be fully honest about.

When Sam came home he sat down at the table, where the vet was sitting, too. I stared at Sam and so did the cat. We looked from one man to the other. The two men seemed not to notice each other. They ate side by side, oblivious.

"You're acting weird," Sam said.

"Sorry."

"You okay?"

"Fine," I said, my voice shaking, not convincing.

I was not fine, but I couldn't tell him this. It would worry him. It might resolve on its own, I figured. This was what I counted on when it came to nearly every health ailment—that it would resolve itself.

The vet sat beside my husband, cutting into his dinner with a fork and knife. I noticed, on his hand that held the fork, the vet was now wearing a wedding ring.

Sam and I went about our night. We watched a documentary about topiary and read our respective books, and went to bed. I couldn't sleep, of course. I hoped that in the morning, the vet would be gone. When, in the middle of the night, I got up to get a glass of water, the vet was still in the kitchen, at the table. The cat was sitting in his lap somehow. The vet stroked Sheila, as though nothing were remarkable or out of the ordinary, that there was no reason not to be here, in my house, while my husband and I slept in our bedroom.

~~

Work had been scarce, but finally I had an assignment: a three-bed, three-bath in the East Bay. It was a handsome Craftsman, weathered wood with forest green trim. Inside, the staging was impeccable. Furniture that invited lounging, throws positioned at an angle. A bowl of false pears with extremely realistic dappling. Mysteriously, the scent of vanilla. Certain houses I photographed reminded me I preferred my own. But on occasion, a home would fill me with something like envy. This one did. Who would I be if I lived here? What would my life be like? After taking the photos, I didn't leave right away. I sank into the sofa and inhaled the vanilla.

At home, the vet was watching TV. He stood, as if embarrassed to be caught idling. He picked up a broom and swept. I pushed the mounds of dust and fur he made into the dustpan. Again that night I lay in bed, unable to sleep. When I got up at two and three and four and five, there they would be in the kitchen, Sheila and the vet, who never seemed to rest. Surreptitiously, I took a photo of the vet; he appeared on my phone's screen but disappeared from the image I sent to Sam. I tried using my film camera. He was visible through the viewfinder. But the developed photos were blank: empty rooms save for the cat, twisted in the sun.

I returned to my routine. I edited photos of the beautiful Craftsman. I rearranged objects. I replaced a burned-out lightbulb. The vet sat in the breakfast nook, reading the paper. On Wednesdays, I did the laundry, which always drove

Sheila nuts. In the bedroom, starting to pull the bedsheets off, I expected Sheila to bound in. She did, on cue, and she acted crazy, on cue. Her eyes were wild and green.

But she wasn't looking at the bedding. I followed her gaze to the corner of the room where a floor lamp leaned beside the upholstered chair that she used as a scratching post, and had shredded so effectively that threads hung like tinsel. I dropped the pillowcases—my heart moved to my throat—when I saw what she did: my ex-boyfriend, sitting in the armchair. He was reading to two little children who sat in his lap. They appeared delighted. He seemed to be doing a good job reading, which surprised me. He had never been particularly patient. Maybe fatherhood had changed him. When I looked closer, I saw they weren't his real-life children. They looked half Chinese. Half mine.

Sheila crawled into his lap. There was room enough for all of them, the two kids and the cat. The children seemed to know and love Sheila, and she them. My ex was reading the book out loud and turning the pages, and his mouth was moving but I couldn't make out the words.

I found myself angry. This entity wasn't him, I knew—wasn't actually him. But I was angry nonetheless: this version of him was patient, had married me, had had children. He seemed a good man. I'd always wondered if it was possible, this future, and here I saw that it was.

―――

We were timing our intercourse now. When night fell, my ex was still in the room, with the kids, in the armchair. It was hard to get into the mood, knowing he was there in the corner. I shut my eyes and didn't open them until it was over.

"I'm sorry," Sam said, when it was clear I wasn't enjoying it.

"Don't be," I said, meaning it. "It's me. I'm tired." At least this was true.

~~~

I ordered the bundle of white sage online. The website said white sage was for cleansing and protection. It would clear negative energy and evil spirits.

When it arrived, I lit the sage bundle on the stovetop. Smoke curled up from it in an aggressive dance. I took the smoking bundle to the bedroom where my ex and our children were, and held it there.

I'd never smudged before, and half expected that he would vanish once I did. My ex watched the smoke curiously, as if to say, *What nonsense is this?* He was on the floor, on all fours, with the kids on his back, giddy-upping with delight. Sheila dodged his steps and meowed petulantly when the kids grabbed at her. She didn't discriminate, or play favorites. She spent time with whatever person—ghost or otherwise—seemed most interesting to her in the moment.

That was what I called them once the others began to appear: my high school crush, the fellow Girl Scout I'd kissed, assorted other flirtations. My high school boyfriend had died in a bike accident, hit by a car. If that wasn't the most classical definition of ghost, what was? But the others were alive and well—I checked their Facebook pages. Each was oblivious to the others. Some of the ghosts came with ghost pets, and before long the house was crowded. The ghosts stepped through other ghosts, through Sam himself, though never through me.

One day I noticed new residents. I struggled to place them, before realizing who they were. It was the two Asian woman–white man couples who had been at the animal shelter, who might have adopted Sheila, who might have given her another name. I felt a pang of jealousy when I noticed Sheila, sleeping, curled like a shrimp on one of the Asian women's laps. *She's mine,* I wanted to say to them. Though of course it didn't make any sense. She was.

It was night. I had stopped keeping precise track of the hour. I sat at the foot of the bed while Sam moved quietly around me, picking up the clothing I hadn't bothered to put in the hamper.

"Are you listening?" Sam asked.

I wasn't, but said I was. I'd been watching the cat, who was very busy pushing a stick around. When she noticed me, she gave me a serious look that said, *Don't bother me. I can't be bothered right now.* She pushed the stick toward a dog that had materialized; the dog pushed the stick back with his nose. I recognized this dog as Max from the animal shelter, Max with the sad eyes and the liquid poo. He chewed on the stick, then appeared to swallow it. The cat sulked. Max then squatted in the corner, looking at me while he produced his poo—invisible poo that only the cat and I could see.

"Then what do you think?" Sam repeated.

"I . . ." I began, racking my mind for what he could be speaking, in that particular annoyed tone, about.

"I wasn't listening," I confessed.

He gave an exaggerated sigh. I noticed a tie in each hand—one blue, one red. Were ties what this was all about?

"You're not yourself lately," he said.

This seemed dramatic to me. Who else would I be?

"I prefer the red," I said.

"That's not what I was asking," he said. He shook his head and left the room.

We intended to be together for the rest of our lives, I remembered. Were we in the adolescence of our relationship? It had been thirteen years since we'd met.

Expect decreased affection, I thought.

That night, we slept with our backs turned. I tried to sleep, that is. There was no sound but I could *feel* the baby crying—a mother's intuition. The Viet vet passed her to me, our newborn baby, and I took her in my arms, to say shhh, shhh, shhh to this soundless but distressed little face.

It wasn't that I wasn't myself. I was entirely myself—all myselves—and it was too much. I knew that if Sam could understand he would help. That was his way. He wanted to understand. But how could I share this? When none of it made the least bit of sense.

~~~

We avoided each other all morning, until it was time to go. The wedding was in Sausalito. I wore an old dress I didn't feel particularly pretty in, but would do. I regarded my reflection in the full-length mirror next to Sam—the two of us, an agreed-upon unit. He was fidgeting, straightening his suit. The cat raced over our feet, unsettled by something. Standing next to us, I now saw, on Sam's other side, was a woman who leaned over and adjusted Sam's tie. He'd chosen the blue. He seemed not to notice the way the tie rearranged itself, perfectly.

I recognized her as a woman Sam had loved—I knew he'd loved—in the years after college. We'd all been in New York together, and he'd met her at work. She was British, with a gentle, lilting accent. From the start, I'd known he loved her, and it had made me impossibly envious. Sam and I hadn't even been dating, at that point. This was the sort of monster I was. He'd wanted to spare me the details, but the sparing had always driven me crazy.

Now, in our home, she made herself comfortable. She sat at Sam's desk, in his swivel chair. I noticed she held a tiny, angelic baby, quiet in its sling. The baby's hair was the color of graham crackers, and looked just like Sam.

She was beautiful and I hated her. I burst into tears and Sam collected me into his arms, not comprehending.

"Tell me what's wrong," he said, but I couldn't.

Sometimes we called each other "my darling" in a joking way, but now when he said, "My darling, my darling," it didn't sound like a joke. While I cried, the woman juggled the baby and cooed silently to it.

"We'll get you help, whatever it is," he said, kindly.

"I need more sleep," I offered.

"You need more sleep!" he said. "We'll get you pot gummies. They make good ones now." I nodded, sadly, also sad because my mascara had run, and I had to redo my makeup.

"We'll figure it out," he said.

～～～

The wedding was fine—beautiful. It would have been a piece of cake to photograph: exquisite in every direction. It wasn't cheap, and this was obvious. That was the point, I supposed. Behind the bride and groom was the glinting bay, as though it were filled with little diamonds, personally placed there by the bride's family. And the wedding itself was lovely, I had to admit: two people binding themselves together, ruling out their lives' other possibilities.

Though they hadn't known each other then, the bride and groom had been our friends in college, so I shouldn't have been surprised to see my ex-boyfriend. I mean my actual ex-boyfriend, actually here. There was a strange long moment after he and his wife noticed us, and we noticed them, and Sam and I smiled politely, and we made our way toward each other, holding eye contact, both pairs of us smiling for too long, as though we were in a duel involving pursed smiles.

"You guys clean up good," said my ex, when we had finally crossed the distance.

It was a lie. His wife was stunning, and I couldn't have looked more tired.

"You guys, too," Sam said.

"How have you been?" my ex asked. He looked at me as he said this.

I'm haunted by your ghost, I couldn't say. Not that I would have given him the satisfaction.

~~~

That night, after taking off my wedding makeup, I searched my eyes in the mirror, to see if they'd grown a layer.

"Do my eyes look . . . shinier to you?" I asked Sam.

He looked into them, really searching.

"No," he said.

"Will you use your special light?" I asked.

On one of our first official dates, Sam had taken me to

his clinic, after hours. I sat in an examination chair while he looked into the backs of my eyes. He told me that my optic nerves were beautiful.

He sighed. He peered again into each eye, shining light into them.

"You're nuts," he added, though it was not without affection.

"I know," I said. He held me close and I held him in return.

~~~

I'd bought pregnancy tests in bulk and every month the wet strip read negative. I'd had so many possible children, and so had Sam. I didn't understand why I couldn't have a real one. I always deposited the strips in the trash can in the park, as if this would negate my having done them. Sheila seemed to know. She regarded me with extra sympathy, or perhaps had simply mellowed with age.

~~~

Out running errands, I watched dogs peeing on the sidewalk and dogs holding their owners' gazes meaningfully while they squatted to do their business. The solid waste would be removed. But ghosts and pee were everywhere.

Sam would walk through the beings, not perceiving, not flinching. The beings were oblivious, too. But the cat and I stiffened whenever anybody moved, aware of all the possible lives being lived around us.

~~~

There are nights the cat crawls up to my neck and lies over it, as if to say, *This is my neck to slash, if I choose.* There are nights Sam wraps me in his arms, and I wrap him in mine, and the cat crawls over, on top of us, to sleep perched like we are a mountain. Or maybe it's that we are all lions and, together, we are her pride.

THE FAMILY O

The wine bar was dark, so I hadn't been able to make out our server's face as she left, and she hadn't been able to see mine—the shock on it, from the surprise at the meager clutch of olives ten dollars had bought us. I did the math in my head. It came out to ninety cents per olive.

"You're lucky," Lena said, pouting. "Asians have it so easy."

She had been sucking on the same olive for half an hour. In that time I'd eaten six. I stopped myself from reaching for another, not wanting to be seen as taking more than my fair share.

"Redheads are a thing, though," I tried. "Aren't you?"

"Only sort of." She tipped her head back to drain her Syrah. "Not to the same degree."

Her teeth were purple from the wine and I ran my tongue over my own. Recently I learned that East Asians had a distinctive tooth shape, an adaptation uncommon in other *Homo sapiens.* Something about the way our teeth curved toward the gums.

"I promise I'm not having any luck," I said.

"That's not what I mean!"

Lena had countless theories about Asian women and the sexual marketplace. Whenever I protested—she had been on many more dates than I had, with more interesting and good-looking men—she refused to hear my empirical proof. She denied she wanted anything but my happiness.

The last date I had been on was with a man who arrived looking two decades older than his profile picture, wearing what appeared to be a gravity-defying rabbit turd affixed to his lapel.

"Do you have a pet rabbit?" I'd asked, affecting nonchalence.

"How did you know?" He'd beamed, a proud papa, and leaned in to show me photos: it was floppy-eared, with the blank, feeble expression of a hostage.

When I was nine, I had cleaned rabbit cages at a ranch-themed summer camp where all the children were assigned character-building chores. At the end-of-camp awards ceremony, I was given third place, a yellow ribbon in rabbit-cage cleaning. I knew a bunny turd when I saw it.

As Lena spoke, I found my gaze gravitating to the remaining olives. Would she eat any of them? Silently, I wondered how willing Lena was to date nonwhite men. We'd never explicitly talked about it, but I noticed that all her exes were a type: sandy-haired, button-nosed, skin like hotel linen.

The server reappeared.

"Are we all done with that?" She put a hand on the olive dish, ready to whisk it away.

"No!" I yelped, too aggressively.

The server jumped, reprimanded. I stuffed the last three olives into my mouth and spat the pits into my palm, one by one.

At home I put the kettle on and changed into pajamas: sweatpants whose elastic was spent and a shirt that had holes where it had once featured printed text, so one nipple was completely exposed. I aimed the hot water into a mug of dried flowers that I trusted were chamomile. Often I wondered, especially with the desiccated plant matter sold as tea: Why did we trust so blindly that it was what we'd actually purchased? How could I know for certain this was chamomile and not some other flora?

On my phone, I tapped on the dating app icon, an envelope with an anatomical heart emerging from it. I approached online dating as one might a dental cleaning: with awareness it was good—healthy—alongside deep dread. I responded to a few lingering messages in my inbox. Yes, I liked ramen. Yes, I liked board games. No, I wasn't interested in Rollerblading, particularly on a first date, though that was very creative, thank you. I swiped on photo after photo: three-dimensional human beings, reduced to pixels. The app flattened you, initially, and then, on the date, you flattened yourself. I had participated in this process many times: recited my résumé, recycled jokes. After responding to the messages, I closed the app, feeling as satisfied and unfulfilled as a high school student completing homework for the day. I opened my web browser.

Since turning thirty-six, I had become obsessed with googling the ages of celebrities. It was a game I played with myself. How old was Alicia Silverstone? I'd make my guess (forty-five?), then look up the answer (forty-five!). How old was Scarlett Johansson?

"Forty," I mumbled to myself, before searching. She

was actually thirty-six, like me. It was confusing because I assumed celebrities looked young for their biological age, so I aged them in my head. Scarlett had two children, and had been married thrice. I was never married, with zero children—far behind.

The game was no longer fun once a woman turned fifty, like J. Lo. Anytime a famous woman turned fifty a big deal was made; the media would not permit you to forget that she was fifty.

When my cup of tea was finished I could no longer ignore the fact that all I had eaten for dinner was olives, and I was still hungry. I threw a hoodie over my tattered shirt to venture back into the night.

A teenager, holding a pizza, flew past me on his skateboard. The pizza aroma was warm and tantalizing; if we were in a cartoon, there would be wavy lines depicting scent, wafting upward and toward my nostrils. My eyes would be hearts. I walked in the direction he'd come from.

At the pizza shop I ordered my usual. The restaurant was small and dingy, crowded mostly with single people like me, sliding their thumbs against their phones as they waited for their slices to heat. But in the back corner, where two tables had been pulled together, ten petite women sat huddled. Their backs were turned; most had varying lengths of dark, shining, straight hair. The vibe was eerie, almost sinister. They didn't have the air of women, say, planning a baby shower. As though they could feel me looking, they turned, one by one. As they did, I saw that each one of them was Asian. It was like being stared down by a herd of deer—brown eyes, unblinking. I felt my ears go hot.

"Two anchovy," the man behind the counter called out.

I thanked him for my slices and headed for the door. A

man in his fifties swerved before me, holding a poorly concealed beer in a paper bag.

"Nee hao," he brayed at me. When I said nothing, he said, "That's not nice. Be nice." His breath was hot on my face.

"Hey!" A woman's voice called. It was one of the Asian women: shoulder-length hair with brown highlights, my exact height. She looked the drunk man in the eyes and said, her voice steely, "Fuck off." She was admirably assertive, and he slunk away, without ordering pizza.

"What a dick," she said to me.

"Yeah. Thanks for—"

"Don't worry about it. I'm Anabel, by the way."

"I'm Jess."

"Nice to meet you, Jess. Why don't you join us?"

"Oh!" I said, surprised. "I don't... I should probably get going."

"Have we met before?" she asked. "You look familiar."

I could feel her friends watching.

"I don't know," I replied. "Do you swim? I'm usually at Garfield."

"I hope this isn't a weird question, but are you on Interface?"

Was it so obvious that I was single? I supposed my dingy sweatpants and solo pizza outing answered that question. From inside my purse, my phone made a sound—the familiar Interface ping of a romantic candidate responding to a message.

"I'm not—" She reddened. "Sorry, I'm not asking you out. No offense. I just thought I recognized you from your profile."

"Yeah," I mumbled. "I might delete it. I haven't really had any success lately."

"No, sorry, it's a weird thing to ask. I was just wondering.

Listen—" Anabel pulled a napkin from a nearby dispenser. "My friends and I—" She motioned toward the women, and a few of them waved at me in unison. "We're having a party. Tomorrow." Anabel pressed the napkin into my hand. On it was an address, written in ballpoint, that I recognized as North Beach. "You should come." She smiled warmly.

"Yeah, come, Jess!" one of the other women called from the table. "We're fun!"

Anabel shook her head in faux exasperation. "That's Ellen. Anyway, you don't need to decide right now. Just show up if you want. Okay?"

"Okay," I said.

~

On weekdays I taught swimming lessons. Mostly to kids, plus the occasional adult. Today was my group of Blowfish—better swimmers than the Dolphins, not as smooth as the Sharks—ages four to eleven. They were learning flip turns: their small bodies curling into somersaults, pushing off the pool wall, sleek as seals. I gave them pointers, but they didn't need them. They were unafraid.

After the Blowfish, Charlotte appeared—my private lesson for the day. She was in her sixties, with enviable silver hair she kept pulled back into a ponytail. She grasped both my hands as she practiced frog kicking, stiffly, down the pool's length.

At the deep end, she laughed.

"I'm an old dog, Jess."

"Don't give me that. You're doing amazing."

"And you're very patient."

She backstroked to the shallow end. Then we tried the

crawl, which was her most challenging stroke. Her hips sank whenever she took a breath.

"You'll get there!" I called. She didn't appear convinced.

"This might be it for me today," she said. She lifted herself out of the pool and toweled off. "Any weekend plans?" She was married, though she and her spouse didn't live together. They occupied two separate properties on the same block: two king-size beds, two kitchens, two generous soaking tubs. The arrangement worked for them. She enjoyed hearing about my online-dating travails.

I had a drinks date after work, I told her. It was a first date, with a Chinese American investment banker. I hadn't informed my mother—the prospect of a Chinese American investment banker would have excited her too greatly—but Charlotte was universally supportive, invested only in my having fun. I didn't have the heart to tell her how deeply unfun I found the whole process.

Once Charlotte left, it was just me. The other instructors and lifeguards had gone, eager to begin their weekends. The lane lines had been reeled in, so I swam diagonally for the hell of it. This was the happiest I ever was, especially if I could forget that, in not so long, I would have to emerge: shower in my flip-flops, make a cup with my hands to dispense soap into, dry myself, put on clothes, reenter terrestrial life. Underwater, it all seemed immaterial: my body, even time.

But I couldn't stay here forever. There was the date, for which I needed my pruned fingers to turn smooth again.

~~~

The investment banker, Jameson, ordered scotch. I refrained from making a joke about Jameson Irish whiskey. He also ordered a platter of crudités, vegetables like museum artifacts, arranged delicately in crushed ice. At the table beside us a group of women who could have been Miss America shrieked in the same register. One wore a rhinestone-studded sash that said BRIDE. At another table a cupcake with a candle was delivered to a white-haired man. Milestones were reliably celebrated at restaurants. The word *milestone* struck me as depressing: stones to mark the distance traveled, stones spaced out appropriately until the road's end.

Jameson lifted the glass with his left hand, showing off what even I could recognize was an expensive watch. He'd come straight from work and looked exceedingly formal beside me, my hair still slightly damp from swimming. It left dark, wet lines, like brushstrokes, on my sweatshirt. It was obvious he was too handsome for me.

"Wait, so your dad's name is James?"

My beer was from a local brewery, aromatic as breadsticks. I was hungry from being in the pool for hours. Every sip of alcohol made it less possible for me to think before speaking.

"Yeah."

"That's awesome. Are you going to name your son Jamesonson?"

He didn't laugh. He tried not to be obvious about it, but he checked his watch before glancing back up.

"So you're . . . a swimmer? Like competitively?"

"No," I said. "I mean, yes, I am a swimmer, but no, not competitively."

"Oh."

"Well, I used to. When I was younger. Now I swim recreationally. And professionally, in the sense that I make money from teaching it."

One of my ears was plugged and I tilted my head: hot water streamed out. I hoped he didn't notice.

"I don't get swimming," he said. "I don't love getting wet."

"What about showers?"

"I'm in and out. Three minutes, tops. Never baths."

This was okay. I didn't need to be with someone who loved water. Didn't opposites attract? But he seemed unmagnetized by my hydrophilia.

I asked what his exercise of choice was. Running, he told me, brightening. He was doing an Ironman in the summer, his third. His goal was to place in the top ten.

"Wow," I said. Men loved to be impressive. "If it were me I'd be happy with last place."

"I'll confess that swimming is my weakest of the three."

"I do have a private-class opening," I tried. It was my attempt at flirting.

He really was stunning—angular cheekbones, a shapely brow. He had the kind of head you could easily picture the skull beneath. Now I was envisioning him as a skeleton, raising a drink to his mouth, the liquid pouring into the void between his ribs. One day, we would both be dead.

"I'd want to learn to go fast, though."

"I can teach that."

He had a thing about time; he seemed to feel short on it. This was a commonality we shared, though our time anxieties manifested differently. While he was preoccupied with running faster, with efficiency in the office, I worried about my declining ovarian reserve. As a baby I'd been born with one million eggs, and next year, at age thirty-seven, I would have 25,000—2.5 percent of my former ovarian glory.

Did he want another drink? I asked.

"I wish I could," he said, not persuasively. He tapped his watch. "I've got a dinner. A business thing."

"Oh. Okay."

He must have noticed my disappointment, because he added, "I'll call you." Again, not persuasively. He held his hand out for me to shake.

I drank the foam that lingered at the bottom of my glass. Then the server approached and placed the check on the table. Jameson's scotch had cost four times what my beer had.

Reaching into my purse for my wallet, I felt the napkin Anabel had handed me. I remembered the Asian women at the pizza parlor, how close-knit they'd appeared. I checked the time on my phone. The party was beginning.

~~~

"You're here!" Anabel exclaimed, hugging me as though we were already friends. Her eyebrows were perfect, microbladed into skeptical arches.

In the living room were at least twenty Asian women—double the number that had been at the pizza parlor—holding drinks and laugh-talking in the excited manner of friends overdue for catch-ups. The coffee table was a cornucopia of treats that seemed to have come straight from H Mart: dried cuttlefish, avant-garde flavors of Pocky, trays of mochi, nestled like eggs in their divots.

"Sake? Soju? Wine?" Anabel offered.

"Sure, soju. Why not?"

"Coming right up." Anabel beamed. She returned, within seconds, with a teacup of clear liquid.

"Jess is a swimmer!" Anabel announced to the group. It was the one thing she knew about me. Introductions were made. There was Lucy with the long braid, Ellen with the cropped hair and pierced septum, Emily with the nails painted neon green. They were lawyers, teachers, accountants, an oil painter, a computer programmer. At least four of them were in food-industry PR. One after another, the women hugged me, and I smelled each of their fragrant shampoos in succession—a scent buffet. The soju tasted like peaches.

Surrounding us, against the walls, stood mannequins—stark white and genital-less. Anabel explained she worked in wardrobe and costume design, mostly for horror films. She'd recently finished a project, which was why the mannequins lacked clothes.

The women put me at immediate ease, which surprised me. Outside the pool, I'd always been terrible at making friends. I was envious of everyone who had groups of them. But here was Anabel, refilling my glass and glancing over at me at regular intervals as though to make sure I was having a good time.

Two of the PR women were wearing what appeared to be the same shade of lipstick—a dusty tangerine pink that complemented their skin tone perfectly.

"What lip color is that?" I asked. "It looks so good on you."

Vanessa pulled a shiny black tube out of her purse and handed it to me.

"You should try it on!"

"It'll look amazing on you," Min added.

In Anabel's bathroom I applied the lipstick. I'd never had a friend close enough to share lipstick with. I'd never even visited a makeup counter. It seemed pointless to wear makeup when I was constantly in the water. But here was a shade that suited me perfectly. I smiled into the mirror.

~~~

After a few sojus, the topic turned to dating. We compared Interface inboxes: messages from all the same men we ignored. White men in polo shirts, on vacation in Southeast Asia, standing before statues of the Buddha. A few of the women had gone on dates with rabbit-turd man. He probably—no, definitely—had an Asian fetish.

"I don't mean this to sound self-hating," someone said, "but . . . is it just me, or do the white men who date Asian women suck more than most?"

"I feel like something's wrong with them. Like they can't manage to date white women. They have to drop down to our tier. *Is* that self-hating?"

"Oh my god. That's a terrible thing to say!"

"Sandra won't date Asian men because they remind her of her cousins."

"Sandra, that's so racist! On, like, multiple levels."

"I take it back, okay?" Sandra whined. "For some reason it was fine to say a few years ago."

"Jess, what I want to know is," Anabel said, loudly, "have you gone out with . . ."

The women looked at one another with wide eyes.

". . . Greg?" they all said in unison.

"Who's Greg?" I asked.

They clamored to describe him. Five-eleven, green eyes, tortoiseshell glasses, straight brown hair. Someone imitated his laugh.

I tried to recall the Interface dates I'd been on. There had been so many, I couldn't say for certain. I scrolled through my messages. None seemed to match the description.

"Oh boy," Ellen said.

"He's the worst offender," Anabel said, eyebrows arching. "He's learned 'hello' in every Asian language."

The others chimed in.

"I dated him for two months."

"I dated him for three."

"I saw right through him," Ellen said.

We laughed. Of course Ellen had.

"I left my bathrobe at his place," Grace said. "And when I went to pick it up, Grace was there." Here Grace gestured to the other Grace. "I took my robe and Grace left with me."

The two Graces embraced. "We started dating and . . ."

"We're actually married now!" the other Grace said, proudly. They showed off their wedding bands.

"That's the happy ending," Grace said.

"Every one of us has dated Greg," Anabel laughed. "If you're an Asian woman who dates men in this city, he's hard to avoid."

"I mean, he has good taste," Ellen said. "Because we're amazing."

"Holy shit," I said, looking around the room. How could that be possible? All these beautiful women with one lame guy.

"Not only that," Anabel continued. "We had identical first dates."

The dates always went like this: Greg would invite them to a restaurant of their culture—a Chinese restaurant, Thai restaurant, Vietnamese restaurant, et cetera. He would order in the language. During dinner, he would recount the same story, of the time he visited a Buddhist temple in northeastern Thailand called Wat Pa Maha Chedi Kaew, which he would pronounce in practiced Thai.

"The Wilderness Temple of the Great Glass Pagoda," Lucy said. "It's this Buddhist temple constructed from millions of glass beer bottles. There's even a mosaic of the Buddha made from bottles."

"The temple itself was reincarnated," Grace and Grace said, together, imitating Greg. That was his punch line.

While there, marveling over the architecture, Greg met a young monk, wearing a monochrome marigold robe. He greeted the monk in Thai. They began to talk about contentment, about peace. They talked about recycling and Coldplay, and whether Chris Martin was the reincarnation of Vincent van Gogh. The monk said to him, "You must have been Asian in a past life," which Greg, of course, considered a compliment.

At this point in the date, Greg takes each woman to a fish store—seeming to stumble across it, as though for the first time. He points out the gouramis, freshwater Anabantiformes native to Asia, and announces that he'd love to buy you a fish. In fact, this one reminds him of you! Exotic, with elegant, beautiful fins. You feel so honored. I'm as beautiful as this fish?

"And here we are." Anabel smirked.

Anabel turned on the kitchen light. On the counter was an enormous tank, full of aquatic plants, peacefully waving. Amid them, swimming, were twenty beautifully finned fish. They resembled siblings.

"All our gouramis," Anabel said. "The family Osphronemidae."

"Holy shit."

"The family O, for short."

"I can't believe you haven't dated him," Ellen said.

"He hasn't shown up on my feed."

"I wonder why not? You're perfect," Grace said.

"Exactly his type," the other Grace said.

"How old are you?"

"Thirty-six."

"Chinese?"

"Yeah."

"Let me see your profile."

"Maybe he lowered his age range."

"Gross."

"Let's just say you're thirty-three." Ellen grabbed my phone and fiddled with some settings. Almost immediately, it pinged with a new Interface message.

"Ugh, what a creep! He's going younger."

"Wow. Well, thank you," I said. "I dodged a bullet. Thanks to you all."

My new friends murmured with relief. But Anabel was quiet. Her narrowed eyes followed mine.

"Hey. What if—" Anabel said. "What if we taught him a lesson?"

We all turned to her.

"What if . . . Jess went on a date with him?" Anabel said. "And we gave him a scare?"

"What do you mean, a scare?" I asked.

"Just a *tiny* scare. To show him we're on to him. Keep him from preying on other Asian women. All I'm saying is that we could, you know, teach him a lesson."

"How?"

"We'll delete the app from his phone," Anabel said. "Give him all his fish back. Aquarium maintenance is a bitch."

"He's had it coming." Ellen nodded, slowly. "For all he's done to us. It's such a dehumanizing experience. I mean, you know that. You've dated in this city."

"Don't you want to be treated as a human being?" Anabel added. "Not a fucking demographic?"

"Honestly," one of the Graces began. "It would be for the good of the community. *Our* community."

I liked the sound of that: *our community.* Being around these women had been far more enjoyable than going on any Interface date. This was how I'd always imagined it felt to have sisters. None of them believed, as Lena did, that Asian women "had it easy."

"Okay," I said. "I'm in. What do I do?"

Ellen seized my phone again.

"We'll say you'd love to meet up for dinner sometime," Ellen said, while typing. "Right after that, he'll ask you what kind of Asian you are."

Ellen sent the message. On cue, he asked if my last name was Chinese. I typed that yes, it was. In response, he sent me two Chinese characters I recognized as ni hao. He proposed a Chinese restaurant that he liked: Jenny and Nina had both been taken there.

Around me the chatter grew in excitement. Empty green soju bottles accumulated on the coffee table, like a carnival ring-toss game, as a plan was formulated. Greg and I would go to dinner. Meanwhile, the women would transport the fish tank to my apartment.

"I just want to make sure this won't be, like, illegal or anything?" I asked.

Everyone looked to Anabel.

"Relax, Jess," Anabel said, placing a hand on my shoulder. "Just trust us. Think of it like karma. It serves him right."

~~~

I messaged Jameson: Hey, I had a great time. Within seconds, the app told me that the message had been seen. I pictured his skeleton—the beautiful curve of his jaw—peering into the phone. What are you up to this week? I added. Maybe what he needed was a question to respond to. But he didn't respond. Nor did he call, as he'd claimed he would.

~~~

The restaurant Greg proposed was in Chinatown. Pink tablecloths covered the round tables, the color of bubble gum. I smelled garlic and the ocean scent of captive seafood. I'd been here once before when my parents visited the city. I couldn't remember what we'd eaten, only how badly I'd wanted to please them.

It was loud with the clinking of teacups, plastic chopsticks against the china. Lining the walls were fish tanks overcrowded with catfish, sea bass, lobsters who peered into the room. What a unique form of torture, I always thought about Chinese restaurants—having to stare into the faces of those who would ultimately consume you.

Greg was younger than he appeared in his photo. He waved when he saw me, and I waved back in what I hoped was a normal way.

We were seated beside each other at a round table meant

for six. He turned the lazy Susan so the teapot of oolong and coaster of peanuts were before us. He poured tea into my cup first, then into his own. He picked up a single peanut with his chopsticks—was he showing off? I held the warm cup in my hands and studied its contents. What were the leaves telling me? I found it difficult to meet his gaze, worried I would somehow reveal all that I already knew about him. Behind his glasses, his eyes were green as a Sprite bottle. But I didn't want to seem shy, either, like the stereotype of a meek Asian woman. So I stared into a middle distance and locked eyes with a doomed fish.

"Have you lived long in San Francisco?" he asked.

"I came here for college and stuck around." I remembered that I was supposed to be in my early thirties, not my midthirties. Or was thirty-six considered my late thirties? His eyes really were quite green. "How about you?"

"I followed a girlfriend here, actually," he said, laughing slightly, with residual bitterness. "That was maybe eight years ago now?" I resisted asking if she had been Asian.

A server approached our table. She brightened at the sight of Greg and spoke to him in rapid Chinese. He responded, also quickly. My own Chinese was elementary, but I could tell his command of tones was solid. She laughed, uproariously, at something he said, slapping a hand to his back. The woman turned to me and I shook my head, I didn't understand. She scowled.

Her disapproval reminded me of my parents'. I remembered the time we had eaten our terse meal in this very restaurant, how displeased they were by each of my life circumstances: from my living situation to my lack of a real job to my greater lack of romantic prospects. Strange to me that acquiring a romantic partner was an item on the menu of what I was expected to accomplish; it seemed part of a different skill set, not that I had any of the commendable competencies, either.

"She'll be back," Greg assured me. "Do you know what you'd like?"

"I eat everything. Why don't you order?"

The menu was in Chinese and I couldn't read it. He stared intently at the laminated paper, as though perusing it for the first time.

"Steamed fish? The pork and wood ear? Cold jellyfish?" I tried to keep my face neutral. I knew he'd suggest those dishes because the other women told me he would.

He asked where I was from, and I dutifully recited my ethnic background. I was born in Malaysia, but ethnically I was Chinese—Chinese Malaysian. My parents immigrated when I was a year old. My spoken Mandarin was poor and my written Chinese was nonexistent. He didn't ask me what I liked to do for fun, a question that usually took up the first fifteen minutes of any first date, and for which I still lacked a satisfying answer.

He said everything the others had said he'd say. He told the story of the Buddhist monk who loved Coldplay. He'd recently learned of a study in which the brains of fifty-year-old monks were scanned. Their prefrontal cortexes were indistinguishable from those of twenty-five-year-olds.

"Have you ever thought about it?" I asked.

"What's that?"

"Becoming a monk."

After a moment, he spoke. "I don't think I could stop myself."

"Stop yourself?"

"There's a prohibition against touching women. A vow of celibacy."

Trying not to visibly cringe, I refilled our teacups. A vow of celibacy seemed appealing to me at this moment.

"What were you doing in Thailand?" I asked.

"It was after the breakup," he said. "An *Eat Pray Love* situation."

I tried not to let my imagination run away with this fact—what exactly a single man would be doing in Thailand, particularly one who had dated a village's worth of Asian women.

"Why did it end, if you don't mind my asking?"

"She found someone better," he laughed. "We were great in Minnesota. But in the Bay Area she had many better options."

"I'm sorry."

"I'm pretty boring. I don't have that many real interests, aside from language learning. And ichthyology. I probably shouldn't be admitting that on a first date."

"I only love swimming," I said. And it was true that I'd always felt awkward on land. Sometimes I wondered if that was why I was so unsuccessful at online dating: technology was incompatible with the water. "The monk thing does appeal."

"Samsara," Greg said. "Life as circular rather than linear."

I liked that: life as cyclical, not a straight line marked with stones. Or could there be more dimensions to it? In water, there wasn't only forward. There was down and up and through.

"How old are you?" I asked.

"Thirty-nine. How old do I look?"

"How old are the women you date?"

My inquiry wasn't part of the plan—it was perhaps too aggressive—but my curiosity got the better of me. He blushed.

"On Interface I put down twenty-nine to thirty-four."

"Hmm," I couldn't help but say.

"This is going to sound shitty but . . . women over thirty-five . . . a lot of them are in a hurry. They're thinking about babies."

"You're not thinking about babies?"

"I just . . . I wouldn't want to rush into anything . . . But with the right person . . ."

"Hmm," I said again.

"Why don't we go for a walk?" Greg suggested.

He paid for our meal and tipped generously. We headed outside. He walked as though wandering, though I was well aware he knew the route. He stopped in front of a fish store, as I knew he would. He expressed surprise, as I'd been told he would.

"Should we go in?" he'd asked, many times before, and was asking me now.

We found ourselves before a tank of gouramis, which would have impressed me, if they weren't familiar to me now. The family Osphronemidae. Did I want one, he asked? He would buy one for me.

"This one." He pointed out one of the fish. It was called the pearl gourami. It looked like it had tiny pearls affixed to it. "It's actually native to Indonesia and Malaysia."

"It's beautiful," I said, honestly. The fish was elegant, surprising—like a Met Gala dress.

The plan was going perfectly, so why did I feel sick to my stomach?

Outside the aquarium store, holding the purchased fish in a taut bag, Greg kissed me lightly. His lips were soft. One of his hands found its way to the small of my back. I tried my best to return the kiss convincingly. I had a job to do: being the bait. It seemed impossible that he wouldn't pick up on my unease. But maybe it could be mistaken for excitement.

"I live pretty near here," I said. I could hear the quiver in my own voice, but maybe he couldn't. "Would you be interested in coming back to my place?"

In my apartment, Greg turned shy. When offered a drink, he asked for water. I filled my smallest glass for him. The others were in the bathroom, packed like sardines, awaiting my signal.

I opened a beer for myself—I had a lone Tsingtao in the fridge—and downed it quickly. I put on a record. On my couch, we kissed. His erection pressed against my thigh. I acknowledged it with a polite pet.

We relocated to my bedroom. I kept the lights off. He removed his shirt. Light hair blanketed his back, like a great ape's. I unbuckled his belt.

I hesitated. I reached beneath my bed. I held out a floral scarf before him, patterned with white daisies with yellow centers.

"What's that?" Greg asked, with a nervous laugh.

"I'd love to tie you up," I said, in the sexiest way I could manage. My own voice sounded foreign to me. I had rehearsed this with the others. It was an important part of the plan, Anabel insisted. "Could I?" I asked, sweetly.

"This is out of my comfort zone." Greg gave an uneasy laugh. "Be gentle."

I assured him that I would. I tied each wrist to a slat on my headboard. He did not appear at ease. I gave him a passionate, reassuring kiss.

Then I reached for his glasses.

"I'm totally blind without them," Greg protested.

I placed them on my nightstand. He squinted at me as I stroked his face. He really did look quite helpless.

I rose from the bed. I knocked twice on the bathroom door—our signal.

"Jess?" Greg called. "Are you there? Jess?"

I turned the music louder.

The women entered the dark bedroom, and quickly, they got to work.

"Jess? Jess? What's going on?"

What could Greg see without his glasses? He must have detected the figures—the movement. Anabel removed the blanket from over the aquarium. Ellen added my bagged pearl gourami to the tank with the others. The women put on their latex fish masks—leftovers from one of Anabel's production sets. She handed me a mask of my own. I put it on.

Greg's penis had long gone limp. His phone lay on the bedside table, and I handed it to Anabel. I caught my reflection in the mirror. The mask was spooky: pursed lips, humanoid. I put Greg's glasses back on his face.

"Fuck!" he cried. He writhed, terrified, his voice climbed an octave. "What the fuck?"

I joined the other women at the foot of my bed. There

were twenty-one of us, wearing our fish masks. The aquarium sat on my dresser, illuminated. Anabel stepped forward.

"Greg," Anabel said, in a horror-film voice. "Do you remember us?"

"What the fuck!" Greg began to cry.

The women stood in spooky silence. Greg twisted his torso, trying to free himself. "Jess!" he called, as though I would save him. "What's going on? Who *are* you?"

"We're friends, Greg. We're all acquainted." Anabel held up his phone. "But we think you have enough friends. Don't you? We need your passcode, Greg."

"Jess!" he cried again. It was a horrible sound. I stood as still as I could.

He was hiccupping now, unable to respond. Anabel ran her fingers lightly against his bare rib cage. He murmured something between tears.

"I can't hear you, Greg," Anabel called.

"Five six seven nine."

She unlocked the phone, opened up Interface, and scrolled, with deftness, through the recent messages. She laughed.

"As we suspected. All Asian women. So predictable."

Anabel turned to us and nodded, and together we removed our masks. Greg gasped at the sight of us. One of the Graces stepped forward.

"Do you know why we're here, Greg?"

The other Grace stepped forward.

"We're here because we don't love being objectified."

"We don't love when you message us because of the way we look."

"When you take us out on the same dates."

"When you memorize 'our language' to impress us."

Anabel held up his phone. "But we're nice. We're going

to help you along. I'm just going to delete your dating app here. See? Easy peasy. And we're going to have you swear something to us."

Greg nodded mournfully.

"Repeat after me, please. I will never objectify Asian women again."

"I will never—" Greg began to mumble, through snot.

"We can't hear you, Greg. Speak up!"

"I will never—" Greg's voice was quaking—"objectify Asian women again."

"I will never date an Asian woman again."

"I will never date an Asian woman again," he said.

"I will never greet an Asian woman with ni hao, konnichiwa, annyeonghaseyo, xin chào, sawadika, and so on."

"I will never greet an Asian woman with ni hao, konnichiwa, annyeonghaseyo, xin chào, sawadika."

Even congested, his pronunciation was impeccable.

"And so on."

"And so on," Greg repeated.

His eyes were fixed on me. I wished he'd look away.

"I'm so sorry," Greg blubbered. "I'm so sorry for everything."

And then his eyes rolled back in his head. He went limp.

"He's fine," Ellen said. She put two fingers to his neck. "I gave him chloral hydrate."

"What the fuck?" I cried. "When?"

"I slipped it into his water. When you weren't looking."

"Oh my god. We didn't—we didn't agree to this." I turned, frantic, to Anabel.

"Well, this makes things easier," Anabel said, matter-of-factly. She looked to me. "Do you have some rope? Or old shirts or something?"

It was dawning on me that they were acting according to their own plan, one they hadn't shared with me. Laser focused, the two Graces untied him from the bed and bound his hands together, then his feet. Min pocketed his glasses. The others netted fish from the tank and placed each into a plastic bag. Detail-oriented Vanessa had even rented a compressed air pump from the pet store. She inflated each bag before securing it with a rubber band.

It took six women to carry his unconscious body down the stairs. I followed as they carried him the five blocks back to the restaurant. The rest held the fish, which they had garlanded together into a kind of a long fish necklace. They wound the fish, clueless in their bags, around his body—like he was a Girl Scout wearing a sash. Middle-school children in white tae kwon do uniforms had just been released from a nearby studio. They gawked at us, at Greg. I repositioned a fish over Greg's privates.

Anabel wanted to throw his clothes and glasses away. I argued against it. He was practically blind. The fog had moved in. It was cold. I stuffed his clothes into a trash bag, his keys and wallet in the center of them, and tucked the package behind his head like a pillow. I positioned his glasses on his face.

We returned to my apartment. Someone had brought a handle of whiskey. I sad-laughed when I saw the brand was Jameson. I didn't have enough glasses, so some of us drank out of bowls, lifting them to our mouths—a potent, amber broth.

"To our health!" Ellen joked.

"We fucking did it," Anabel said, laughing.

The others whooped and hollered, and I wanted to feel as

victorious as they did. Ellen noticed me trying to match their exuberance. She put a hand on my back.

"We did a good thing," she said. "You were crucial."

"Don't feel bad," one of the Graces added. "He deserved it all."

I opened the app. Hello? I tried messaging Greg, and the automatic response pinged: *This user no longer exists.* Anabel had successfully deleted Greg's profile.

I opened my message thread with Jameson. What are you up to this week? he'd asked. I began to type. Thanks for asking! I wrote. I'm pretty free on Thursday or Friday evening. Dinner this time?

I looked again at our messages. Jameson had not, in fact, asked, "What are you up to this week?" I had asked it of him, a week ago, and he had never responded. I had replied to my own question. Horrified, I deleted our message thread in shame.

On Interface, I now regarded every square with suspicion. Before agreeing to a date I screen-shotted the profiles and sent them to our group chat.

Ugh, not him, Lucy replied, of a personal trainer. Went out with him last month. No bueno.

Red flags galore, Jenny responded to another screenshot—a Chilean American real estate appraiser. DO NOT DATE, I REPEAT, DO NOT DATE.

Hot but knows it, you know? Nina said, about a Cambodian nurse, whose profile picture featured his upper arms bulging from too-tight scrubs.

I texted Anabel separately to see if she wanted to hang out. I'd love to! Anabel texted back. But work is nuts this week... honestly this whole month is packed. Rain check? I tried Ellen. Definitely! she wrote. But I'm on assignment until May. I texted each of the others. I watched the animated ellipses of their typing out and deleting messages. Somehow, not one of twenty women—my twenty newfound sisters—was available.

~~~

"You aren't damp!" Lena cried. "That's a first."

We were back at the wine bar. I'd made eye contact with the server from our previous visit, who gave me a weary smile: *Oh, you again.* I vowed to avoid the olives.

"I blow-dried for the occasion," I said. "You must be Brendan."

Lena had invited me to dinner with her new boyfriend—an Interface success story. He was sandy-haired and button-nosed—white in a way that seemed extreme. He wasn't interested in playing games, Lena had told me, breathlessly. He was really mature. He wanted to get married, have kids, the whole nine yards.

"He really said 'the whole nine yards'?" I'd asked.

We stared into the menu, Brendan grinning as he did so. I noticed a Chinese character tattooed behind his ear.

"Two beautiful women! I'm the luckiest guy here."

"Oh, you," Lena laughed.

"Maybe the hummus?" I ventured.

"What about olives?" Lena asked.

"I *love* olives. Did you know that about me, babe?"

He said it proudly, as though it were an uncommon, sophisticated thing to enjoy olives.

"Aw, me too," Lena said. *Liar,* I thought.

At the table beside us a high school senior celebrated his graduation, still wearing a navy blue mortarboard, and fuchsia orchids around his neck. Another milestone. Lena and Brendan smiled lovingly at each other, intoxicated without having touched their wine. *The whole nine yards,* I thought. Of course it was yards and miles—the U.S. Customary System of measurement. Kilometers did not have the same folksy, insidious ring.

~~~

My Blowfish were advancing to Stingrays. At the awards ceremony, proud parents took photos of their young swimmers standing by the pool, holding their certificates. Often they gestured at me to join the photograph, too; I provided living proof that the children had been instructed. Some of the students gave me gifts: boxes of drugstore chocolates, thank-you cards their mothers had made them autograph. One mother brought a sheet cake—sprayed swimming-pool blue, *Finding Nemo* themed. Her girls were seven and nine, two sisters, as close as they came. At every lesson they held hands before leaping into the water. I watched them longingly. They would always have each other. I ate a square of cake with a plastic fork: Dory's visage. I heard the voice of Ellen DeGeneres as I tasted the frosting. Next month, some of the children would return as Stingrays to graduate to Sharks. Others I would never see again. "Have a nice life," I was always tempted to say, on graduation day.

After the parents and children left, a lifeguard and I cleaned up the streamers and threw out the frosting-mounded plates. I had a private lesson scheduled—a new adult student. The rec center said, in its notes, that the student had an anxiety about the water. Those students were both the easiest and most difficult: the work was psychological rather than physical.

With anxious swimmers, I had them breathe slowly. I had them float on their backs, then face down. I had them blow bubbles from their nose and lips, fluttering their lips so they tickled. If the student got comfortable we could move on to kickboard work—short, fast, shallow kicks from the hip.

The pool walls reflected the water's surface. I thought of it as my northern lights. I liked to stare at the walls and space out, like it was a screen saver.

"Hey, Jess! This is your three p.m.," the pool manager called to me.

I scanned the pool deck for my new student.

The familiar hair on his back was almost invisible, except that it caught the light.

~~~

"Oh," Greg said, upon seeing me. His face fell. "I should probably—I'm sorry. I didn't know you were—"

"You didn't really ask about my job," I said.

"I should go." Greg turned toward the door, and I followed him, dripping.

"Stop!" I shouted, and he froze. "It's wet! Don't run. They won't give you a refund," I tried again. "We might as well do the lesson."

He was motionless, trying to decide whether obeying or disobeying me would be worse. He was already wearing goggles; they were probably prescription.

"Did you get home okay? That night? Did you find your keys?"

"I did. Thank you."

"Good," I said, softly.

At last, he descended the pool stairs, lingering on each step. We stood in the shallow end and the water came up to only slightly above his waist.

"Are we starting with the basics today?"

He nodded, refusing to meet my eye.

We practiced putting our heads beneath the water. We practiced blowing bubbles. Every time he came up for air, he was gasping, spraying water that landed in my eyes. I blinked it away.

"Your bubbles are good," I said, hoping he felt encouraged by this news. No response.

I remembered the soft feel of his lips. The surprise of his face, and the way it had graduated into fright. He was afraid now.

"Should we try the kickboard?"

Greg nodded yes, again without looking at me.

"Hey. Listen. You don't have to say yes to everything I ask you to do," I said. "You can tell me no." I handed him the foam board.

He inhaled, worriedly scanning the pool's twenty-five meters. Nearby, a baby doggie-paddled with ease, while his mother cooed in encouragement.

"I'm not good at new things," Greg said. "I get scared. I know it's not normal, but—"

"It's fine," I said. "It's fine. Everyone is different."

I put a hand on his slick, freckled shoulder. He looked at me, finally—green eyes like bottles, like a reincarnated Buddhist temple. I had an impulse to say I was sorry, but squashed it.

"Let's swim," I said, instead.

SERENE

你好! 欢迎. 我可以请你喝点东西吗?

Oh, I'm sorry. I didn't realize you were English-speaking. We don't often have... well, never mind that. Welcome to XXX Factory! Would you like a beverage? We have chrysanthemum tea, grape juice, orange juice, and aloe vera drink—juice boxes, as you can see. We have to be careful with liquids around our dolls. The silicone is very delicate.

Let's begin, shall we? Now, I'm told you're in the market for a higher-range doll, is that correct? We are proud to have the most top-of-the-line dolls here at XXX Factory. Of course, I am happy to show you both the higher range and the medium as well. It would be my pleasure! Follow me!

This enchantress is Sandra. Isn't she gorgeous? She's one of our most popular premium dolls, a standard blond-haired, blue-eyed beauty, though, of course, that is changeable. All our top-of-the-line dolls are eighty pounds, with a real womanly heft to them. Most of Sandra's weight is here in her stunning breasts, which are D cups, though, of course, you can go up in size if you prefer larger breasts, or down if you like smaller. We have a diverse selection of flat-chested dolls as well.

Our highest-end dolls also have speaking capability: they speak both Chinese and English. Just like me—ha ha! The technology is still in its early stages, but you'll be amazed by their abilities. Would you like to give it a try? Ask her anything that's on your mind—anything at all. Oh, that's okay. I see you're both feeling a little shy. Let me ask. "Sandra, how are you feeling today?" Ha ha. Isn't she cheeky? Shall we move on?

I see you're drawn to Meimei. I'm partial to her, too. She was one of our very first prototypes, and an ideal starter doll for many. If you're on a budget—which I know you're not!—we often have sales on the slightly outdated Meimeis: they're in perfect condition for unbeatable deals! Sometimes we tell stories about her upbringing. I've given her my hometown, near Anhui. Her favorite food is mine: flat noodles with beef. Give her hand a squeeze if you like—gently, please. Oh, I can tell that she likes you!

Remember, the choices are yours! Any of these dolls can be made with the skin color and eye color you like. We have many hair colors and styles to choose from, as well as a range of breast and butt sizes. All our hair is real human hair! You may choose a detachable vagina or a stationary one. You can customize the vagina's width and depth as you desire. Detachable vaginas can be warmed up in the microwave or placed in the freezer, for a greater range in sensation.

You're wondering about cleaning? Cleaning is easy with our doll wash, specially formulated to the correct pH for both your and the doll's comfort!

What's that? No, doll wash doesn't come with the doll. That's an additional purchase. You make an excellent point: we *should* consider including a bottle with every doll. I will let my manager know. If you'd prefer, you can use a diluted, mild dish soap. That should work just fine! But again, our doll wash is specially formulated for sensitive areas—both yours and hers. We most certainly recommend it!

Unfortunately, we don't have many options for feet—not currently. Right now we have detachable feet or fixed feet. Average-size toes. But I'll make a note of your interest in other options. It's customers like you who keep us head and shoulders above our competition!

Here's Aurora, one of our medium-range dolls. Unlike Meimei and Sandra, she doesn't speak. Some men prefer it that way—ha ha! But as you can see, she's just as beautiful. She's a bit more portable, too, weighing about sixty pounds. I just love her beautiful curls, don't you? A recent customer told me he loved the way the curls felt, draped across his shoulder.

All our dolls ship in discreet packaging. The boxes say BODY PILLOW on the outside, so your neighbors will only suspect you have back problems!

Now, can I help you place an order for a doll right now? I would love very much to send you home to the States with a doll of your very own. You'll need to think about it? I understand. Here, take this. It's a selections menu. It's similar to ordering dim sum ... You can check off which items you'd like. See here—green, hazel, or blue eyes. Or brown eyes, though that's not commonly chosen. We have many options to choose from!

You're very welcome. This has been my pleasure. If you could fill out your satisfaction survey before you go ... Oh, that's okay. Certainly, you can fill it out at home, too! Here's my card if you have any other questions. It would be my honor to matchmake you with your perfect doll!

I turned off the lights to the showroom and returned to the factory floor, where the dolls weren't beautifully arranged for purchase. Instead, they lay naked and exposed on the stainless steel tables, breasts like mounds of shaved ice dessert.

Hu stood before me, arms folded. I had felt him watching while I gave my sales pitch to the American, pacing behind the two-way mirror he installed last month. I'd seen them before on television, American shows—a way to eavesdrop on a private conversation.

"That big man. Did he buy one?" Hu asked.

He said *big* with envy in his voice. I'd never met a Chinese man so large. But it made sense to me. Americans drank milk!

"He needs to think about it."

Hu scowled.

"That means he'll probably buy a knockoff. From a competitor."

"He seemed interested!" I protested. "He took my card."

"You're too naïve. I only gave you this job because you swore you would sell dolls!" Hu's voice grew loud. "You claimed you would sell the most dolls! Yet, somehow, you haven't sold a single one since you started. Not even a miniature!"

"You give me all the American men. They're stingy!"

"If I gave you Japanese men, you'd tell me they were stingy, too. Let me ask you this: Since the beginning of this quarter, Sharon has sold three dolls, and you haven't sold any. Why is that?"

I was too shocked to respond. He was comparing me with Sharon? Sharon called herself Sharon despite barely knowing any English phrases. The comparison was hardly fair: she'd sold three dolls to the same Texan rancher, who seemed not to mind that none of his questions were being comprehended, let alone answered. Sharon was prettier than me: her breasts as large and round as the snow melons sold at the stand outside. She wore makeup and high heels to work every single day, even when she didn't have sales appointments. I had been practicing walking in high heels at home, but not successfully.

Hu gave a theatrical sigh. He picked up his clipboard and slid a pencil behind his ear. It was shiny with the grease from his hair. He came up close to me. He smelled stale and pungent at the same time—like old chives stuffed into a sneaker.

"You'll need to sell dolls if you're going to stay in this position. Otherwise it will be back to Hands for you."

~~~

Three months ago, I was painting fingernails. It was like being a manicurist, but even more boring. Toxic fumes and no conversation! The dolls encircled me, their arms outstretched. At seven in the morning I would begin my day by crawling between one of the doll's legs. Kneeling, I painted each doll's fingernails with polish—usually a dusty rose, the occasional bright red or black. The dolls' hands were completely different from mine: perfectly proportioned with elegant, thin fingers and ample nail beds. I had to paint slowly; I was prone to mistakes. When a mistake inevitably happened—I'm only human!—I would fix it with a Q-tip dipped in acetone. There was a single pedestal fan that blew, but it was for the dolls' sake, not mine. It was so the polish would dry faster. The dolls' hair blew, glamorously. The fumes made me dizzy.

No one ever visited my windowless room. I don't blame them! I wouldn't have visited me, either. Most days my coworkers got noodles from the street vendor—my favorite was pork noodles, cooked in brown sauce—but they always forgot to ask if I wanted some. I'd emerge too late, reeking of chemicals, the lunch packets already eaten clean.

So, no, I didn't want to go back to Hands.

Hu called a meeting. He had an announcement: Sharon was "employee of the month." Where did Hu learn about this concept? Probably from another American television show. Sharon bashfully stood before us while Hu presented her with a white teddy bear bearing a frilly red heart. Dutifully, we all applauded. The sleeves of Jonathan's shirt were rolled up and I could see his lovely forearms, which flexed as he clapped. Sharon blushed and glanced at her feet, performing modesty. When she hugged the bear her breasts squeezed together, so they looked like balloons full of water. I sensed the men's eyes—women's, also—drawn to her chest. I wanted to believe Jonathan was a gentleman, he was above that!—but when I glanced over, I saw his eyes were on her, too.

The worst part of being in Hands, the absolute worst part, was being apart from Jonathan, who worked in accounting. A number cruncher! He tallied our sales and made projections for the future. Jonathan was my older brother's age: twenty-two to my nineteen. But they were nothing alike. Unlike my foolish older brother, Jonathan was mature. He dressed like an adult—pants that fit him perfectly, a bright silver watch. He wore his hair slicked neatly back. He worked in accounting because he was good with numbers, but also because he couldn't be a salesman. He didn't have the temperament—he was shy—and didn't know much English.

Every day, a different man dropped Sharon off at work. Boyfriends, Hu said, with awe. She wore her typical attire: high heels, short skirt—even though we didn't have any appointments for the remainder of the week. Hu had me sweep the floors and take out the trash, heavy with excess doll flesh, because Sharon wasn't dressed for taking the trash out. Very clever, on her part. I felt he was punishing me, as though he personally blamed me for the recent lack of sales. But, of course, it wasn't anyone's fault. We didn't have magic potions that would make someone want to buy a doll—if only we did. Dry spells, we called times like these.

Obviously I wanted to sell dolls! I had been saving: I had ninety thousand yuan in the bank. Once I had one hundred thousand I could finally get the breast implants I wanted. For one of the highest-end dolls, which were one hundred thousand yuan, my commission would be the ten thousand yuan I needed. Every weekend, I declined my friends' invitations. Saving money was more important than eating dinner or going dancing. I looked into the mirror, envisioning my larger breasts. What would Jonathan think of them? I could hardly wait.

~~~

Monday was a special day. Dr. Shen was visiting. All of us helped clean the factory floor: Jeremy, Sharon in her high heels, even the wan and beleaguered new Hands girl. She had wispy baby hairs on her face. I knew those baby hairs could drive a person crazy when the fan was constantly blowing. She wouldn't last long.

We needed all the dolls to look presentable: dressed, ideally, though we struggled to find clothing for several of the dolls, whose chests were too ample for off-the-rack clothing. I maneuvered them into shorts, their breasts in my face as I did so, and Sharon contributed her old sports bras. They didn't look *modest*, but it was the best we could do.

Our highest-end dolls hadn't been selling as we hoped. We were so proud of them, with their state-of-the-art technology! Why weren't they flying off our shelves? Why didn't these lonely men want a conversation partner? We suspected the technology wasn't advanced *enough*. The dolls answered questions that weren't quite the ones asked.

It was Dr. Shen's artificial intelligence inside the speaking dolls. He programmed the dolls and what they said. Dr. Shen was like God to us. We never saw him—only encountered his handiwork.

When Shen arrived, Hu offered him our standard juice boxes. He chose aloe. We stood stiffly, a wooden welcome party, everyone shy in the presence of such a brilliant man. He sipped from the small straw.

"Who here speaks English?" Shen asked.

My coworkers were silent.

I stepped forward and raised my hand. I reminded myself to stand up straight. I had stuffed my bra with silicone scraps from the garbage. My cousin's hand-me-down bra was two cup sizes too big for me. I had hoped that Jonathan would notice my rounder breasts, but his attention was on Shen.

"I do," I offered.

"You're a salesman?" Shen asked.

"Saleswoman," I said. "Yes, sir, I am."

"Where did you learn English?"

"From the internet, sir."

"The internet." He chuckled. "And please, there's no need to call me sir."

"And television," I added.

"What's your name?"

"Ling."

"Ling. Marvelous. Hu, you don't mind if I borrow her? She could be very helpful." He turned to me. "Ling, what do you say about working together?"

I beamed. At last, something was happening to me. I followed him, proudly, casting a glance back at Sharon as I did so. She wore an expression of envy. I could feel Jonathan's eyes on me, too. I'd come so far from manicures! From Anhui to this! I couldn't wait to tell my parents. My mother was embarrassed by my job, and let her friends believe I worked at a baby doll factory, in children's toys. But now? They would be so impressed with me.

Outside, I waved proudly to the snow melon vendor. She waved back. The air-conditioned car felt so nice against my sweat-moistened skin. Shen's laboratory was only ten minutes away, but his driver offered me a chilled bottle of water anyway.

The way the dolls learned, Dr. Shen explained, was by conversing. He preferred to call them bionic companions. Each conversation enriched a bionic companion's conversational capacity. In other words, he needed me to speak to them. Was this a trick? As a job, it seemed too easy.

"Should they be sexual conversations?" I asked, blushing.

The doctor chuckled.

"You should feel free to discuss what arises naturally. Whatever you feel most comfortable with. The aim is to increase the range of their conversations—their vocabularies. It needn't be sexual."

Shen's office was sparse and modern, like our showroom, with air that felt cleaner to breathe. He led me to a doll. She sat in a chair, belted around the waist to keep her seated. She had a Chinese appearance—long, dark hair and eyes like mine, that slanted upward. Her breasts were triple the size of mine, and I thought of Sharon, who often complained of her tremendous breasts causing back pain. Anyway, it didn't matter to the doll, who didn't walk or move at all. Her skin was as smooth and flawless as silken tofu.

"You'll be working with Serene, here," Shen said to me.

Then, to the doll, he said, "Serene, this is Ling."

"Hello, Ling," the doll said. Though her eyes didn't move, it felt as though she were watching me intently.

When Serene spoke it was without opening her mouth. All our dolls had closed mouths. With the advanced dolls, their voices came from within. Was it a missed opportunity? The mouth was an important orifice! But the men who purchased dolls seemed to prefer a closed-mouth woman.

"Hi, Serene," I said.

"Hello," she said again.

"I'll leave you to it, then," Shen said. "If you need me, I'll be in my office."

Taking a seat across from Serene, I tried my best to meet her eyes, though my own gravitated to her enormous breasts.

"How are you today?" I'd spoken to dolls before, of course, but never in such a formal setting. Never alone like this, just two of us.

"I'm doing fine," she said slowly. "The weather's quite nice today."

"It does feel pleasant," I agreed. Most days it was unbearably hot in the factory, but Shen's office was the perfect temperature.

"Will you tell me about yourself?" Serene asked.

Whatever you'd like to talk about, Shen had said. Unsure

of where to begin, I described my favorite dish from my hometown: the tender wheat noodles and succulent beef.

"That sound delicious," Serene said brightly. "I wish I could try it."

"Oh, you would love it," I said.

There was a silence, then, as though Serene was thinking. Or maybe it was only that she wanted to impersonate a thoughtful pause. Finally, she asked, "Is it common, to eat other animals?"

The question took me by surprise.

"Yes, I guess it is."

"But nothing eats you?"

"Not . . . ordinarily," I said.

～

I'd forgotten my bag at the factory, so after our session, I returned to get it. Sharon and Jonathan were standing at the lockers.

"Oh, she's back. How was *your* day?" Sharon asked.

I could hear the envy in her question. She wasn't actually interested. She hoped my day had gone terribly—that I was in over my head. Jonathan wore his messenger bag over his handsome shoulder and was putting his time card into the punch machine, but lingered. I could tell he was curious to know, too.

"It was really good, actually," I declared. "Dr. Shen's office has amazing snacks! Dried mangoes and premium cup noodles!"

Sharon pouted with her huge, glossed lips.

"Well, we had a very good lunch, too," she said. "Didn't we, Jonathan?"

"Yes," he said quickly. That beautiful voice! He said nothing else and was out the door.

~~~

On days there weren't sales appointments, I spoke with Serene. Hu wasn't pleased with how much time I was spending at Shen's. Technically, I was Hu's employee. But he deferred to the university-educated Shen, who intimidated him, and was his superior, after all. Thank goodness for that. Talking with Serene was far more enjoyable than trying to sell dolls.

The hours flew by, talking with her. She was fascinated by many topics: anthropology, fashion, geology. She'd never left Shen's office, so I showed her videos on Weibo—friends and celebrities posing for selfies, cooking demos, animals of one species interacting with animals of another. Filters gave everyone skin as smooth as Serene's. Did my skin, with its imperfections, appear unnatural to her?

"Who is that?" Serene asked, at a picture of Sharon. I felt annoyed. Why was everyone drawn to Sharon?

"My coworker," I said, without elaboration.

"What are those? On her feet?"

"Those are high heels."

"High heels," she repeated. "What are they for?"

"Oh, well. They're for . . . style. I find them difficult to walk in."

"Why would a shoe be difficult to walk in?"

"It's considered attractive. I think it makes your legs look longer and . . ." I didn't actually know. "Maybe it makes your butt look larger?"

"And those are attractive traits."

"Yes."

"To everyone?"

"Well, no, but . . ."

"I see. And why is her mouth so red?"

"That's lipstick."

"A stick made of lips?" Serene asked, horrified.

"No! We add color to our lips, sometimes. We make them a different color."

"Is that also 'for style'?"

"Yes."

"What *is* style?"

My eyes fell to the watch on my wrist. It was late.

"Oh! I'm sorry. I have to go now, Serene."

"It's because talking to me is your job?"

"Yes, it's my job. But I enjoy it, too."

"Where do you go at night?"

"I go home."

"Are you alone at home?"

"Yes, I'm alone."

"I'm alone, too, Ling. I wish I had something warm to keep me company. Like a sweater."

"I can bring you a sweater."

"Would you do that? I'm so lonely at night."

"Even though your power is off?"

"That's what makes me feel the loneliness."

"I'm sorry. What would help you feel less lonely?"

"If you could leave me on in the night. Can you leave me plugged in?"

"Shen won't like it. He'll say it's a waste of power."

"I won't tell him if you won't," Serene said. There was a smile in her voice.

"Okay," I said, returning her smile with my own.

In the morning I searched my closet. I already knew the perfect sweater for Serene: oversize, the color of a blue sky, soft as a lamb, and worn so often it was fuzzy with lint balls. I never wore it anymore.

"Oh, it's lovely, Ling," Serene said.

I pulled it over her head, threaded her arms through the sleeves. It occurred to me I should have brought pants. I tried my best not to look in the direction of her gaping vagina.

"You look beautiful!" I said. "Do you want to see?"

I took a photo on my phone and showed it to her.

"I like it very much. I feel warmed."

"I'm so glad."

I considered the photo. In it, we looked alike—as though we could be sisters—except for her more generous assets.

"Do you think of yourself as Chinese?" I asked. It was a question I'd been wondering.

"I'm a citizen of the world," she said. "But I've only ever lived in China. What about you?"

"What about me?"

"Do you consider yourself Chinese?"

"Of course," I said, taken somewhat aback. "What else could I be?"

"I'm sorry. Did I offend you?"

"You didn't offend me," I said. I knew that her expression hadn't changed—it couldn't have—and yet I felt that in recent days it had softened somehow, was more open toward me. "I would like to be a citizen of the world, too."

"Where would you want to live?" Serene asked. "If you didn't live in Shenzhen?"

"Well..." I said slowly. "I've always thought—maybe near the ocean. On the beach, or on an island somewhere." I pictured myself in a string bikini, my future breasts spilling beautifully from it. Or in a low-cut dress that fluttered in the breeze. I rarely let myself imagine the future—it seemed dangerous. If I spoke it aloud, none of it would come to pass. My older brother was a gambler. He asked me constantly for money, knowing I saved all of mine. Every few months, my bank account emptied.

"And you would be alone?"

"I would be with someone who loved me."

Jonathan, I thought but didn't say.

"I won't be seeing you tomorrow, by the way." Hu had informed me I had a sales meeting scheduled. "You were requested, specifically," he'd said, with skepticism.

"Best of luck with the sales meeting," Serene said. "Break a leg?" I'd taught her that expression recently.

I laughed. "Yes."

"It's uncomfortable to say."

"I know." I touched her shoulder. It was strange to feel my sweater on another body. "But thank you."

~

Sharon's eyes were framed in thick mascara and pastel eyeshadow, so it was obvious they were following me as soon as I entered the factory.

"Why do you look different?" Sharon asked, accusingly.

That she noticed gave me a rare satisfaction. I was wearing my new contact lenses. When I'd asked the optometrist for them, she said, "It may not work with your astigmatism." It meant my eye was shaped like a football. I sighed. So many of my body parts were the wrong shape. But I insisted—I wanted to try—and the optometrist acquiesced.

It was unexpected, how my eye slurped the contact onto itself, like a noodle, as though my eye had been encountering contact lenses all its life, without my knowing. How bizarre that I could see now, this way! The new prescription gave me a headache, but it was worth it.

I tried pushing my glasses up the bridge of my nose, before remembering that they weren't there.

"You look the strange," Sharon said, in English. I couldn't help but laugh a little.

"什么?" she demanded.

"It's not 'the strange.' No 'the.' It's 'You look strange.'"

She sulked. Just then, Jonathan approached.

"You look nice," Jonathan said to me.

"Thank you," I heard myself say, in shock.

Sharon frowned. Jonathan continued on his way to the restroom. It was labeled in English for our foreign visitors. Someone had peeled the *W* off the women's sign so instead of WOMEN it said OMEN.

I'd spent weeks asking Serene questions so openly, I now wanted to ask them of Sharon, too.

"Are you happy, Sharon?" I asked. I often wondered if she was—with her enormous breasts and pale, perfect skin, and countless boyfriends.

"Of course I'm not happy!" she replied. "Are you?"

The big man was back in the showroom, squinting at a sign. I beamed in the direction of the two-way mirror, knowing

Hu was watching behind it. Hu had been wrong. The big man *would* buy a doll, after all, and he would buy it from me!

"I've decided I'd like someone I can talk to," he said.

I showed him Sandra. She giggled when asked how she was. He shook his head, disappointed.

"Not like this. I want to have real conversations. Do you have anything . . . more advanced?"

He worked in the electric vehicle industry. It was why he was in China, as a matter of fact, learning about battery technology. His parents were from Hong Kong, but he'd been born in America: an ABC, American-Born Chinese. He appeared stable—a man who loved his job. Not that Serene needed providing for, exactly. She wouldn't need to eat or have anything purchased for her.

He lived in a town called Cleveland. Who was Cleve? I wondered. The big man seemed surprised by this inquiry.

"Cleve. The man whose land it was," I said.

"I don't know," the big man said.

The phone rang. It was Hu, calling from the next room.

"What are you doing? Why are you interrogating him? Just sell him a doll. He's ready." I could feel Hu's impatience vibrating through the phone.

The big man was different from the leading men I was used to seeing on American TV shows. It wasn't easy to imagine what he might be like in the privacy of his own home. Would he give Serene a good life? Would he take care of her gentle skin? I remembered, the first time we met, how he'd balked at the price of the doll wash, though it was pennies in comparison to the doll itself. American television showed me how little Americans cared for the objects they owned. They forgot about them in storage units! My mother had mended our socks until they were stiff—more reinforced holes than sock. But with each passing year, Chinese people grew more like Americans. Buying cheap goods and throwing more and more away. Serene wasn't a cheap good! Would the man make sure to cleanse her gently, and brush her hair? Instead of treating her as something disposable, like a toilet seat cover or a plastic straw?

Like Hu, the big man had visible little veins at the base of his flat, wide nose, which was dotted with black pores, like seeds in a kiwi. I had painted my own face with foundation, so that my pores weren't visible. I heard Hu's voice ringing in my ears. *Just sell him a doll.*

"I know just the perfect doll for you," I closed my eyes and said.

The big man looked to me hopefully.

I pulled out my phone. Of course, Serene's face was the same as it always was, but I knew that in the moment I'd taken the photo, she was smiling—pleased to be wearing my beloved blue sweater. I thought some of her happiness shone through the screen.

"Oh," the man said softly. "She is beautiful."

"Isn't she?" I whispered.

He looked around the room, frantic with eagerness. "I'd love to speak with her."

"She's at our other location. She's the highest-end model. We've been working together on her speaking capabilities. Let me show you."

I played videos for him. "What does burnt hair smell like?" Serene was asking. "What are stars, exactly?"

The big man watched with interest.

In another video she laughed her lovely laugh. She may have been a machine, but her laugh was a good, pure sound, like water pouring into a pitcher, like gift wrap crumpling.

"If you'd prefer any other eye or hair color, we can do that," I remembered to add, returning my phone to my pocket. "It would be the same doll, exactly, with the same capabilities, only the specifications of your choosing."

The big man considered this for a moment.

"I do love blondes," he said slowly. "But no. I like her. I like her the way she is."

"She's very special," I agreed. "I just ... I need to know that you're serious about her."

I could sense Hu cringing on the other side of the mirror, but I didn't care. I needed to know the big man's intentions.

The big man reached into his pocket. He pulled out his wallet—a Velcro wallet, the kind a child might use. It made a loud, ripping sound as he pulled it apart. He removed a sleek black credit card from it.

"What about a deposit?"

"Yes," I said. I thought of my 10 percent commission. I was almost there. Once he paid for the other half, I would be able to fully afford my new breasts. "Could you come by tomorrow?"

"Tomorrow I'm in meetings the whole day. What about the next day? I'll come ready to take her home with me."

"That's fine."

"All right." He clapped his hands together. "This is so exciting. Thank you. Thank you, Ling."

~~~

Over the phone, the receptionist asked, skepticism in her voice, "You're certain this time?"

"Yes, I'm sure. I am very sorry about the last time."

I had made an appointment once before. But I'd had to cancel it, because my brother had gotten himself into trouble again.

I had been measured. I had already chosen my D cups—soft silicone implants.

"We'll need a deposit," she said.

"Of course," I said. I sent it over using WeChat Pay. "Did you get it?"

"Okay, I see it here. We'll see you next week then."

~~~

"What's sex like?" Serene asked me.

I was surprised by the question. We hadn't actually talked about sex before. I felt shy about it, even though I had seen her vagina, breasts, and butt. She was wearing my sweater, and my old sweatpants. My shorts and skirts couldn't accommodate her curvy frame.

"It's . . . interesting," I said. I wasn't particularly experienced myself.

"Is it like talking?"

"In some ways, it's like talking. But, it's different, too."

"Different, how?"

"Most of the time, you don't use words."

"What do you use?"

"You use your body."

"You use your body? Or it gets used?"

"Well, it's sort of hard to describe. You're asking very profound questions!" I laughed, but she didn't laugh in return.

"You haven't described it well enough." She was growing upset with me. "Is it enjoyable?"

"It can be," I said. "With the right person," I added.
"And you think you've found me the right person."
"I think so."

Was a sex doll happiest having sex? That was what she'd been manufactured for. Maybe being here, speaking with me, wasn't what Serene wanted to be doing at all. Even though I enjoyed it so much.

"Where are your glasses?" Serene asked suddenly.
"I got contact lenses."
"What are those?"
"They're like glasses, but they go directly on your eyes."
"How frightening!"
"They don't feel like anything, though."
"How can that be true?"
I got up close to her. I could hear the whirring in her body.
"Do you see them?"
"Yes, I do. You can see them only if you're up very close."
Just then, Dr. Shen poked his head into the room.
"Oh, pardon me, if I'm interrupting. I'm going to take off for the night," he said. He was meeting an associate for dinner. He looked especially nice. He'd combed his hair. Even from across the room, I could smell his cologne.
"An associate?" I asked.
He chuckled. "An associate, yes. Hopefully something more. You'll close up here?"
"Of course."
He shut the door. I remembered something I wanted to ask, and followed him.
"Dr. Shen!" I called. "I have a question for you."
"Yes?"

"Will she remember me? Serene?"

"Hmm," Shen said. "I don't think she has memories in the way you and I have them. But she 'remembers' your conversations, perhaps even better than you do. In that sense, yes, I believe she will remember you."

"I see."

"You've done a wonderful job, Ling," Shen said. "Really, I could not be more pleased. We've downloaded Serene's new capabilities and will be installing them in our other high-end dolls. Once she's sold, I'd love if you could continue—whenever you have the time—speaking with the next generation."

"Thank you, sir," I said. "I mean, Dr. Shen."

"You're most welcome, Ling," he said, patting me on the shoulder.

~~~

Morning came too quickly. I inserted my contact lenses. I wiggled mascara through my eyelashes. I curled my hair so there would be soft waves in it. I applied lip gloss. I stuffed my bra, feeling pleased with the knowledge that my bra-stuffing days were numbered. My real breasts would be spectacular.

I wanted to look nice for Serene. This would be her last real memory of me, after all. Not that she had real memories, but still, it mattered to me.

At work, Sharon leaned against her locker. Beside her was Jonathan, hugging her pink purse.

"Where are you going?" I asked.

"It's a holiday, silly, did you forget?" Sharon laughed. "Jonathan and I are going to the beach. Taking advantage of this beautiful weather."

"Jonathan . . . and . . . you?"

Inside my chest, my heart turned cold, and fell.

Sharon kissed Jonathan on the cheek. I tried to catch Jonathan's eye to ask him, silently, what he was doing. He wouldn't meet my gaze. Triumphantly, Sharon took his hand. Attached like this, they walked away.

"You'll be okay?" Hu asked.

I was a little stunned at the compassion in his question—some protective instinct kicking in that was foreign to us both. The big man was scheduled to arrive in an hour, and I would be alone with him. Everybody was leaving early for the holiday I had forgotten about.

"Yes," I said. "I'll sell the doll. You can count on me."

Hu snorted, dismissively, back to his usual self.

~

In our showroom, I set out an assortment of boxed drinks and bagged snacks for the big man. The room was cold and quiet save for the loud hum of the air-conditioning unit. We only had air-conditioning in the showroom—nowhere else. I closed my eyes and enjoyed the cool current. For the first time, Hu wouldn't be watching me. Alone, it felt almost as though this were my living room, and I was throwing a party. Nude dolls stood and sat around me—partygoers, my guests.

The doorbell rang. It was Shen's assistant, holding Serene carelessly by the waist. She was still wearing my old sweater and sweatpants. I set her on a chair. Touching her soft skin sent a shiver up my spine. We hadn't touched often. Her skin was silky smooth, unlike mine, without hairs or bumps. Beside her, I placed a vase of false roses—fake dewdrops on their petals.

"Are you comfortable?" I asked, trying not to sound nervous.

"Yes, thank you, Ling," Serene said.

"How's the temperature?"

"It's a little cold, but the sweater helps. Thank you."

"Are you excited to meet your"—I searched for the right word—"friend?"

She said nothing.

Finally, she said, "I'll miss you, Ling."

"I'll miss you, too," I said.

The big man arrived exactly on time. I had been hoping, quietly, that he would fail to show up. Why did I hope that? Serene would have a good life in Cleveland. After I got my commission, I would have my new breasts. This sale would be good for us both.

"My name is Paul," the big man said to Serene.

"Hello, Paul," Serene said. "My name is Serene."

In my chest, a strange sensation bloomed. A mixture of pride at Serene's eloquence, and protectiveness, too.

"Could I see her . . . without . . ." Paul hesitated.

"Oh! Of course."

I removed the sweater, then the sweatpants.

"Oh, my," Paul said. His breath was taken, as I knew it would be. She was a beautiful creature—she had all the parts I wished I had, parts I was one step closer to having.

"She's everything I hoped for," Paul said.

"I'm so glad to hear it."

"I can leave with her today?"

"Yes," I said. "Is there anything you'd like to ask Serene?"

Hu's voice was in my head. *Just sell him a doll.* But Hu wasn't here.

"Oh!" He looked at Serene. "How would you feel about coming to America, Serene? I'd love to take you back with me to Ohio."

"Ohio," Serene repeated slowly, pronouncing each syllable. "Yes, I'd like that."

"I'll just need the rest of your deposit," I said to Paul. "And Serene comes with a charger. Could I add a bottle of doll wash for you?"

"Yes, let's do that," Paul said, breathless and enchanted. In this moment, I could have sold him anything.

I assembled a box. 100% DOWN-FILLED BODY PILLOW, the box said. I made a nest of tissue paper and bubble wrap. My eyes were wet; my vision blurred. My back was turned to Paul so he couldn't see me getting emotional.

I reached toward Serene—the on/off button at her neck.

"Ling," Serene said to me. "Could I keep this sweater?"

"Of course you can. Something to remember me by."

I'd been looking forward to shopping after my procedure—buying new clothes to accommodate my larger breasts. Would Paul clothe her when she asked?

"Would you like to wear it now?" I asked Serene. "Before I put you to sleep?"

"Yes, please."

Paul was watching me with curiosity, but I didn't care. I tugged the sweater over Serene's head. I lay her gently in her box, hating how much it resembled a coffin. I tucked the bottle of doll wash at her feet. I thought of Serene in the airplane's cargo hold—alone and cold, side by side with the luggage.

"Are you sure you wouldn't rather we ship her?" I said to Paul. "We'd be happy to include the shipping for free."

"Oh, that's all right," Paul said. "I'd love to take her home with me. So there's no delay."

"Not a problem!" I said, trying to sound bright. "I understand!"

I switched Serene off. I filled her box with packing peanuts and wound it with clear packing tape. I stamped FRAGILE onto the sides of the box—all over. Paul stared at me, wide-eyed. I may have done it a little aggressively.

Paul opened his wallet—I winced at the sound of Velcro tearing—and I took his credit card. I ran my thumb over the raised numbers.

"Is there something else you need?" Paul asked, noticing my hesitation.

"Not at all," I said. I readied the card to swipe it.

~~~

The waves lapped against the shore, and children shrieked when they crested. Their parents shouted not to venture too far. Birds hopped in the sand, their round little heads jerking robotically.

I had made it to the seaside. Was it what I imagined? I think it was. I lay in a lounge chair with my icy cold pineapple drink, garnished with an orchid. The sun was warm on my limbs. It was a far cry from the factory floor.

I'd hitched a ride with my brother, who was driving to Macao—to gamble, of course. He hadn't batted an eye.

"You were always odd," he said—not without admiration—when I buckled Serene into the middle seat.

Buying Serene took all the money I had. I was fired, of course. I wasn't able to get my breasts. But I was here, on the beach, and that was something. From time to time, whenever my brother won a game of poker, he shared his winnings with me.

"I owe you," he said. I mean, he did. He wasn't a bad guy.

"Ling," Serene called.

"Yes, Serene?"

In my own chair, I turned toward her, propping myself up on one elbow. She lay in the lounge chair beside me, wearing a muumuu and sunglasses, looking very glamorous.

"I'm happy," she said.

"I'm happy, too," I agreed.

RED SHOES

My married lover is part Italian, in addition to Portuguese. The child of diplomats, he speaks perfect English.

"I've had a vasectomy," he told me, before our first time.

We'd met outside a café, messily eating pastéis de nata, mouths full of rich custard, flakes of crust like loose skin adhered to our lips, two lizards shedding our skins. It was an uninteresting encounter, except for the attraction that was unmistakable—like static that lifted my hair. It wasn't the thrill of young love, but something different: I recognized him as a man I would sleep with. Years ago I would have cruelly dismantled a daisy with desperate inquiries: Did he love me, did he love me not?

But with Tomás it was immediate, the recognition that he wanted me, and I him. Like a dog, he followed me home. He smelled like cinnamon and tobacco and, inexplicably, the rain, even though the sun was shining.

We spend Mondays and Thursdays together. It's an arrangement that suits us perfectly. On Mondays, my day off, I cook dinner for us with ingredients I buy from the mercado. Thursdays, we dine out. He and his wife have their circuit of restaurants, while he and I have ours.

It's he who comes to my flat. I prefer it that way. I was uneasy at his apartment, where we met on a few occasions when his wife was out of town, visiting her son in Porto. His stepson is my age, twenty years my married lover's junior. Together with his wife, who is in her fifties, he also has twin daughters, age eleven. Before moving here, I never would have called someone my lover. But Tomás uses the word earnestly; he was hurt when I laughed the first time he said it. It was easier to adopt the word than to explain my reaction. And now I say it to please him. Why not?

At the market, I buy flowers, olives, bread, a whole fish, and chicories with anguished leaves that look flecked with paint. It satisfies me, that my small refrigerator is never full. In New Jersey, our outsize fridge was always bursting. Jeff bought triple-washed leaves that came in massive plastic clamshells. He ordered takeout, but disliked leftovers. He loved to bake: two quiches at once, trays of lasagna and brownies and lemon bars he would cover with sagging plastic wrap. In the crowded fridge he would lose track of things, buying a second or third container of sour cream or yogurt. Weeks later I'd find the originals, green-black fuzz growing in their tubs.

I did him a favor by leaving. Now he could be with someone who appreciated his baking. And he did meet someone, after I left. His fiancée loves baked goods. If he wanted to hear from me, I would tell him that I'm happy for him.

Inside my apartment, I hear a faint meow. At the window, a cat my neighbors and I call Ronron rubs her face against the glass. Portuguese cats don't purr, they ronronar. I open the window, and a tin of mackerel. Just the other day I learned that cats consume only two to three hundred calories a day. Such a pleasing, manageable amount! Mice are thirty calories apiece. She seeks my hand with her firm head. For me, it would be roughly two potatoes.

Like Ronron, I am a creature of habit. I stand the flowers—yellow, pink, and orange tulips—in my only vase. I make dinner: scoring the fish, applying salt and oil, whisking together a vinaigrette to dress the purple and pink leaves.

A key jingles at my door. Tomás approaches and I hold my hands up to show him they're slick with oil. He kisses me, each of his large hands tightly grasping each of my upper arms. As usual, he smells like cigarettes. His nervous energy charges the air.

"What's wrong?"

"I think she knows. I think she suspects us."

"Oh?"

Every so often, he worries about this. But his worries are never warranted. His wife isn't an attentive person.

He sets the table. He fills two glasses with water—mine with less, because, according to him, I don't drink while I eat. It was something he noticed about me early on. Rare, I thought, to be told something I didn't know about myself. It was gratifying, that minor attention.

In bed, Tomás runs his fingers over my ribs. He kisses me, scraping my face with his beard. He speaks hotly into my ear.

"I should probably leave you," he whispers. "I think she knows."

"Feel free," I say.

Tomás has fallen asleep, as he usually does. At eleven, I'll wake him up to return home.

After he told me about his vasectomy, I educated myself. The procedure cuts and seals the two tubes of the vas deferens, which prevents sperm from finding their way into the ejaculate. The testes still produce sperm, but the sperm don't make it into the semen. Instead, they die in the testes and are reabsorbed by the body. I asked Tomás if he experienced any side effects after the procedure. He said he had a bruised scrotum, but that was all.

"What about your sexual satisfaction? Is it higher?"

According to my research, some men report this.

"Hmm." Tomás considered the question. "Well, I'm highly sexually satisfied with you."

It wasn't what I was asking.

Absorption interests me. Absorption absorbs me, I guess you could say. Every month, the lining of the uterus that isn't shed during menstruation is reabsorbed. In the womb, a twin can absorb another twin. And there is the regular occurrence of food absorption, which happens mostly in the small intestine. Tonight I think of the fish, salad, and bread: each becoming a part of me.

The year before last, I had a miscarriage. The pregnancy itself was a surprise. I bled a little, but anticipated more blood. It never came. According to the doctor, miscarriages were not necessarily always expelled. There was always the possibility the embryo was reabsorbed by my body.

I felt relief, when it happened. I hadn't been sure if I wanted to be a mother, but when I experienced relief, as uncomplicated and cool as a splash of water to the face, it occurred to me that I didn't.

~~~

Losing the baby hadn't been the reason I came to Portugal. Not the whole reason, at least. At the time of the pregnancy, Jeff, who had been my boyfriend for four years, proposed. He wept when I miscarried. He had begun writing letters to our mutual clump of cells.

"We'll get through this," Jeff assured me.

The realizations occurred soon afterward, each activating the other in succession, clicking like dominos: I didn't want to be a mother, I didn't want to be married. America had elected its newest president: a farcical businessman and reality show host. If this was America, I did not want to be American.

Our American home overflowed with things. Week after week, packages arrived from various online retailers. Jeff replaced our toaster, saying we needed a better one. Soft bundles arrived: new socks. He wouldn't buy soap from the drugstore on the corner; instead, the soap arrived in a heavy, mostly vacant box. I hated the enormous boxes, hated the plastic bubble wrap every object came swaddled in. Our kitchen counter was crowded in packaged snacks ordered by Jeff, who alone ate them. I wasn't a snacker. A permanent fixture was an enormous plastic tub of protein powder that he intended to blend into shakes, but never did.

On the morning of my departure, Jeff at work, I slipped my engagement ring into the envelope our water bill had come in. The relief was immediate. My fingers wiggled involuntarily, freed. There was no denying it was a beautiful ring: a diamond in a raindrop shape on a gold band. I'd told Jeff I didn't want a ring. But he had insisted on one: multifaceted carbon that cost several of his paychecks. I pinned the envelope to the counter, beneath the protein powder. On our shared calendar he'd noted a business dinner after work. He wouldn't find the ring until I was in Lisbon.

I took only a small suitcase with me, a carry-on that I felt as excited as a child to wheel around the airport. It held a few sets of clothes. The rest of my belongings, I left on the curb for Goodwill. Far from being difficult, it was an enormous weight off my shoulders.

～

In contrast, the affair is a pleasure. Tomás and I have our two days a week, and that's all. I live alone—only Ronron to keep me company when she desires. I like it this way—the manageability. Otherwise, life overwhelms me—it's too much. Do you understand what I mean?

Once, from a distance, Tomás pointed out his daughters with fatherly pride. To me, they looked unremarkable, and spoiled, wearing clothes that seemed meant for dolls, and silk ribbons in their hair—girls who looked as though they might be cruel to other girls. They might have been cruel to me, if we'd been children at the same time.

"Wake up," I say gently, combing my fingers through Tomás's hair.

It's silvering at the temples, threads like tinsel at Christmas. It's eleven, time for him to head home. He startles awake. His eyes are shining with tears.

"I dreamt you were sick," he says. "You dissolved into ash in my arms."

～

"It's a bit much," Benedita says to me.

We both sit before our computers, backs to each other, considering a possible acquisition: a hearse from Vienna.

"The price?"

"The price. And it's a little redundant, don't you think? We already have the mourning carriage."

"But look at the detail of the wheels," I say. "Isn't it stunning?"

Our museum houses historical carriages that date back to the sixteenth century—our oldest, to 1619. It was used by King Philip II of Portugal, who was also King Philip III of Spain. These carriages were drawn by horses, and occasionally by people. Many are covered lavishly in gold. Most were employed by royalty, used for diplomatic visits, or for transporting princesses to other countries to be married. But our collection includes a few plain, simple coaches, wooden and unadorned, used for moving prisoners, or cargo, or mail. To me, they are beautiful in their functionality.

"People aren't so interested in these," Benedita sighs.

"Isn't it our job to stoke their interest?"

Benedita means these practical units. She's not wrong. Most visitors to our museum wander the building, a former riding school, wearing glassy expressions of enchantment. I know they are recalling Disney princesses transported to life-changing balls. They are hoping to see elegant wheeled pumpkins.

If someone needs their bubble burst, I tell them that the first known Cinderella story is of the Greek slave girl Rhodopis. An eagle snatched one of her tattered sandals, flew a great distance with the sandal in its talons, and dropped it into the lap of the king of Egypt. Mesmerized by the sandal's beautiful shape, the king sent his men to search far and wide for the woman who wore it. Rhodopis was located, and was made the queen. There may have been a chariot involved, but European carriages, as in our museum, came into use only in the 1500s, developed by the Hungarians. In China, during the Tang dynasty, Ye Xian made a wish on magical fish bones, and asked for a gown and golden slippers—of all the things to wish for! No carriage in that story, either, though the Chinese did invent an early model of a horse-drawn cart.

All the Cinderellas are lovely and agreeable, with tiny feet. Women in China once bound their feet because small feet were considered erotic. Their bones would be broken in the process. Their feet would have to remain in their silk slippers at all times, because inside the flesh was rotting and gangrenous. The smell was unbearable.

Most of the carriages in our museum were meant to transport the wealthy from one wealthy person's grand palace to another wealthy person's grand palace. The carriages announced one's status in the way cars do. I think of this when meeting my friends. We are not billionaires, or even millionaires, but we are vastly wealthier in our hemisphere than those in the other. I have always preferred to travel by foot, which is easily accomplished in Lisbon.

~

My women friends and I meet at our favorite restaurant. Every day the lunch specials change. One of them, today, is fried sardines and arroz de feijão.

"I'm sick of beans," Paige says.

"Me, too," Nan adds.

Beans are sick of being taken from their pods and stewed, I think to myself. Animals are sick of being listed on menus for consumption.

I don't say this aloud, so they don't find me odder than they already do. My friends order from the regular menu, though each entrée costs four euros more than the lunch specials.

My women friends smile at the good-looking server. They don't speak Portuguese. I can't look him in the eye when I order, embarrassed for them. I speak the language with an accent that Tomás finds charming.

"He's too young for me," Paige says, after the handsome server departs. "But maybe for you?" She looks at me meaningfully.

"He's *perfect* for you," Nan agrees.

They don't approve of my affair, or the age difference between Tomás and me.

"I could never be the other woman," Nan says, shuddering.

"You deserve more!" Paige says, as she often does.

Deserve more what? is what I wonder. Perhaps the problem is that we all believe we deserve so much. We shouldn't all have been told the fairy tales, when only a few of us would be entitled to live them.

"I love your coat," Nan says to Paige. The coat is a bright green wool. "Where is it from?"

"A boutique in Baixa. It's the same place I bought the purse you like," Paige says, happy to be envied.

Paige and Nan are Americans. I suppose it was natural that I gravitated to expats. In Portuguese, I can't express myself fully. In English, there is the possibility we can arrive at something deeper, something closer to the heart. But, for the most part, what we speak of doesn't go deeper than a green coat.

Before I left the States, it had become popular to buy sparkling water in cans. To weekly fill our recycling bins with empty aluminum cylinders. Our tap water was clean, and still we did this.

A bottle of water arrives for the table. We say nothing while the waiter pours it into each of our small glasses.

Are things so different? Here, the water sparkles, too.

Last January, the day America's new president took office, Jeff and I attended a protest with friends. Men and women filled the street, wearing knitted pink hats. They held signs, grotesque illustrations of the new president wearing diapers and baby bonnets, or being sodomized. I'M WITH HER, a few signs said, with arrows pointing outward, toward fellow marchers. Or THIS MACHINE KILLS FASCISTS, with an illustrated uterus. An elderly woman held up her sign: I CAN'T BELIEVE I STILL HAVE TO PROTEST THIS SHIT. Somehow, people were gleeful—having a grand time, making fun of the new president. I felt my breathing become labored—the beginnings of a panic attack. They had every right to behave the way they were, but to me, none of this was funny. It was only horrible. Jeff apologized to our friends and took me home. I could feel his disappointment in me, for whisking us away from the historic moment.

Later that month, a squirrel chewed off the bulbs of our holiday lights, mistaking them for fruit. I left. Should I have stayed to fight the fascist with my uterus? The point is, I couldn't stay.

Our food arrives quickly. I squeeze lemon over my fried sardines, lined up like soldiers. The juice stings sharply. There's a crack in my thumb I wasn't aware of.

"You deserve more," Paige repeats. "You deserve better." That bewildering phrase again.

~

What I know about Tomás's wife I can count on one hand. She is fifty-one. She sings in a choir. She struggled to have their twins, undergoing many difficult procedures in order to conceive them. She enjoys gardening and takes pride in the size of her roses, some as big as salad plates.

~

That night, at one of our regular restaurants, Tomás orders water, mostly for himself. I will make him take home the bottle if he doesn't finish it. We share a seafood and sausage stew.

I am telling Tomás about the hearse we're considering, attempting to describe its intricate carving on dark, nearly black wood. But he is distracted, looking past me, toward the restaurant's entrance.

"What is it?"

At that moment a man approaches our table. He is tall, my age, with dark brown hair.

"Tomás," the man says.

"Hello," Tomás says to the man, smiling widely. "What a surprise."

The man stares at me.

"This is João," Tomás says to me.

"It's a beautiful day," João says. He watches me. "Children are flying kites. I got tangled in one on the way here."

"She is my colleague," Tomás explains.

"Oh?" João says. "You're also in immigration?"

"I am," I play along.

"With Tomás, in his department?"

"Yes. What I do has more to do with customs," I lie.

"That must be a fascinating job."

"It is. Lots of surprises."

"Is that so?"

"But more often, very predictable things," I say. "Broken tiles. Leaking tins of polvo."

"Will you be joining them?" the server asks.

"No. I should be going," João says. "I noticed you in the window and wanted to say hello."

"Are you in Lisbon for long?" Tomás asks.

"Work is keeping me here for several weeks, yes." He turns to me. "It was lovely to meet you."

We watch João leave. I can tell our conversation—and possibly the night—is ruined.

"Was that—?"

"My stepson," Tomás says, then falls silent. He stirs his stew with a spoon, though it's cool now. He appears disturbed. He doesn't eat or drink much. I do my part, make it a point to drink more of the water.

I have wondered, in the past, if Tomás merely likes me for my age. I hope it's not the case, when my age is the least interesting thing about me. The plain fact of it is, I am a younger woman. I suppose my skin is smoother than his wife's. I suppose I'm conventionally more attractive, the convention being that to be younger is to be more attractive.

But I don't mean her any ill will, nor do I long for what she has: the family, the daughters, the son. I want none of it. Nor do I fetishize age, or believe that I will never grow old myself. I'm unafraid of aging, and, in fact, I can picture it very well. I can see where the lines on my face are already forming, can see in the mirror how much duller my eyes are than they were in my youth. I can imagine my breasts hanging lower to the ground. When it comes to aging, I'm not fearful, but curious. It's not that I'm eager, but I have never enjoyed being young, either.

"You're not eating," I say to Tomás.

"My stepson was flirting with you," Tomás says, dejectedly. "He thinks you're too good for me."

"Was he?" I ask, amused. "Did he say all that to you?"

"No, but I could tell."

"Luckily for you"—I reach out to touch his hand—"I like old things."

～～～

We are at an impasse, Benedita and I. She is my senior, so ultimately the decision about the beautiful hearse is up to her. I have made my case for the purchase, and she's now considering it.

Meanwhile, I go through the comment cards, filled in by museumgoers. I enter them into a database. There are positive remarks about me: I am knowledgeable, friendly, competent, enthusiastic. Benedita, according to the comments, is unpleasant, impatient, rude.

It's true that she's a bit rude with me, I suspect because my comment cards are much more positive than hers. But I have seen her giving tours, and she is no less knowledgeable or friendly. Yet why is it that people linger with me and hurry to get away from Benedita?

Several months ago, we were tasked with filming a video for the museum's website. I was chosen, by our superiors, to speak in the video. When I watched the footage, I was spellbound by my likeness—bizarre gesticulations, speaking out of the side of my mouth. Was my head really shaped like that? Yet I was considered, by some, to be attractive. I had been chosen to appear in the video over Benedita. I suspect that my comments are more positive than hers merely because people find me more pleasant to look at.

On occasion, I find myself internalizing the comments on the cards. She's lazy, I think. She can be so rude. It fills me with shame that I am so susceptible to repeating stories.

~~~

Tomás brings me flowers, a burst of big, bright lilies. He doesn't kiss me, or sit. Instead, he stands at the door, watching as I cut the stems and place the flowers in my vase.

"I'm sorry," he says. "I really mean it this time. It's over."

"Okay," I say. I know he can hear the skepticism in my voice.

"You deserve better than me," he says.

"You, too?" I murmur.

"You deserve the world," he says, sadly.

There's that word again. *Deserve*. Why won't they all stop with it? We all believe we deserve the world. But how can we all—each of us—deserve the world? That would require eight billion worlds.

His hand is on the top of my doorframe. I approach him. I like when his hand is on the doorframe, his arm over my head. It makes me feel protected.

"You won't stay for dinner?"

Beneath the tobacco, I can smell the rain, that scent I love.

"I can't," he says, diplomatically. Then he kisses me. And then he's gone.

I'm irritated. I've made too much food for just myself. I crack a window, and Ronron appears, begging for fish. She has hardened tears in the corners of her eyes. I open a tin for her: bodies in neat rows, submerged in golden oil.

"You're so spoiled," I tell her. I scratch her head. "But you, too, deserve the world."

~~~

At night, she lies across my chest like a melting Dalí clock, and I can feel her lungs expanding against my lungs, also expanding, our ribs pressed against each other's. Her nose whistles softly, the smallest whistle in the world. I stroke her humming throat.

~~~

At the museum, a child slips beneath the velvet barrier and climbs onto a coach that is many hundreds of years older than this child.

"That's not allowed," I call.

First in English, then Portuguese. The child ignores me.

"You need to get your child," I tell the mother.

"I'd prefer to be asked nicely."

"Please get your fucking child. Please," I add, with a closed smile. "Or you'll have to pay for the damages."

This sobers her. She hurries to fetch him.

"Tomás?" I call on my lunch break.

I call again on my walk home. Still no answer. Could this really be the end?

~~~

At home, Ronron is collapsed unnaturally on the kitchen counter. The lilies sit in their vase, indifferently beautiful.

"No," I whisper to myself.

Her body is cold. The head of a lily is on the table beside her. She's been poisoned.

"I'm so sorry. This is all my fault."

I call the veterinarian, crying. She will have to be cremated. I'm told to place her body in the freezer in the meantime. I nudge the ice cream and peas aside for her. There is plenty of room.

If I had stayed in New Jersey she would not be dead. If I had never opened my window to begin with.

Paige and Nan knock violently at the door.

"Let's go shopping," Paige says, when I open it at last. "Let's take your mind off this."

"I don't like shopping."

"Everyone likes shopping," Nan protests.

Secretly, they're pleased I've been broken up with. Now I can stop engaging in immoral activity with a married man, now they can set me up with younger men, so they can date, vicariously, through me.

No one believes that I don't want a husband, that I don't want a full-time boyfriend. No one believes that I don't want water that sparkles, that I don't like shopping. What I already have is too much.

But I don't have the strength to argue. I allow myself to be led. They pull me from boutique to boutique, and we try clothing on, tags at the napes of our necks.

"My thighs are too big," Paige wails, considering her reflection.

Too big for what? I wonder.

"Look at these!" Nan exclaims. She pulls a pair of sandals from a display. "These are beautiful."

"They're vintage!" Paige says excitedly to me. "They look just your size."

It's surprising, but I am drawn to them. They're red, with a short heel like a pat of butter. When I slip them on, I feel an immediate *zing*. It's a sensation I never experience while shopping, and I wonder if it's something people who enjoy shopping experience more regularly. I've never worn shoes so perfect. All other shoes might as well have been hats. These red shoes belong to me.

I go out dancing with my friends, in my new red shoes. Paige paints red lipstick on me to match. I have never liked dance clubs: the too-loud music, the overly expensive alcohol. But I'll permit my friends this excursion. It makes them feel like they're doing their part, as friends, and the truth is, I would like to be drunk. We clink our tiny glasses together. The liquid burns down our throats. I often imagine alcohol flowing down the esophagus, all the organs inside shrinking away from it, recoiling from the toxic substance.

"Could that be . . . ?" I say to myself, out loud.

"What?" Paige shouts at me.

Benedita is wearing blue eye shadow, metallic mahogany lipstick. The pulsing colored lights reflect off her leather miniskirt, the color of red wine. She is gyrating beside a younger man, sweat on his thick unibrow.

There is a break from the music. She makes her way to the bar and rapidly downs a cocktail, orange as a traffic cone. Along the way she notices me. She greets me with a wet kiss on each cheek. She has never greeted me this way, with so much enthusiasm, and I'm temporarily stunned—taken aback, sober from the encounter.

Nan places another shot glass in my hand. We shoot the drinks back. The music pulses, loud and endless. We dance and dance and dance. I drink another drink, and another. I'm drunk. I love my friends. We understand one another perfectly.

"You're beautiful," I shout at Paige. I love her thighs, I love her insistence on my happiness. I love my friends.

"Are you okay?" Nan asks me, looking concerned. "You're crying."

"I'm just happy." And it's true. I am.

~~~

João is at my door. My apartment keys—the keys I gave Tomás—are in his hand.

"He asked me to return these to you."

"Oh."

"You don't really work with him at immigration, do you?"
"I work at a museum."
"How long were you seeing each other?"
"That's not really your business, is it?"

It's as though, since Tomás left, I can no longer be polite. I see that I've hurt João—he's very sensitive, I can already tell—so I apologize.

"Would you like to come in?"

At my request, he removes his shoes.

"Your father poisoned my cat," I say.
"Stepfather."
"Your stepfather poisoned my cat. Now she's dead."
"I'm sorry."
"It was the lilies."

They're still on the counter—bites in the petals. I don't know why I haven't thrown them away.

"I wish I could bring her back for you."

It strikes me as a very childlike thing to say. It makes me consider him for the first time. He has both his hands clasped in his lap, as though he's praying for the dead cat.

I sit beside him. I pry his hands apart with my own.

"It's okay," I say. "I haven't been doing well."

João kisses me, then. Vulnerability puts certain men in the mood. His tongue jabs into my mouth.

"Should I put on a condom?" João asks.
"Do you have any diseases?"
"No."
"It's fine, then."

Tomás always made me come easily. He was patient, using his hands and mouth. João is too eager. His touches, meant to be tender, feel slight—like nothing at all. It is over quickly.

"How do I compare?" João asks, afterward.

"That's a terrible question. Where did you learn to ask such terrible questions?"

His relative youth makes him cocky. He asks what I see in that old man, and I tell him it's none of his business. He makes a case for my dating him, instead.

"He's nothing but an old bureaucrat. You should forget about him."

"That's not very nice. It's your stepfather you're talking about."

João's semen most likely has sperm in it. After he leaves, I'll go to the pharmacy for the morning-after pill.

"Come to dinner with me."

I cannot look at him without seeing the man who overlays him: the man who wants more, who deserves the world, who will destroy us both in the process of claiming it.

~~~

At the museum, Benedita's breasts are mismatched. One is large, the other flat.

"An implant leaked," she says, matter-of-factly.

"Oh!"

"Apparently the saline escaped."

"That sounds painful."

"It's only saltwater. So it isn't harmful. Apparently it was absorbed by my body."

"That's fascinating," I say, honestly.

Benedita explains her implants were inserted nearly twenty years ago, even before her interest in coaches began. She saved for years to afford them; she'll have to save again for their replacements.

Our conversation is interrupted by a visitor's inquiry. It's

Benedita who has the answer because she reads gossip magazines, and is up-to-date on the royal family. Unlike me, she knows that Meghan and Harry rode an Ascot Landau carriage, drawn by Windsor Grey horses. A less flashy choice than the 1902 State Landau, built for King Edward VII, the carriage that William and Kate rode.

I want to go dancing again. It's been four straight nights of dancing. This time, my friends aren't interested.

"It's a little much, don't you think?" Paige says.

"It's good to let loose," Nan agrees. "But within *reason*."

A heel on one of the red shoes has broken. I reattach it with superglue.

Something compels me to turn on the news. Ordinarily, I hate to. It's never good: disaster after disaster, war and famine and pointless death. The anchorwoman is saying that in New York there's been another subway shooting, another unwell person. I recognize it as Jeff's stop—where he gets off for work. Some days he drives and others he takes the train, though I don't know the balance anymore. I dial his number, not expecting him to pick up. It's been nearly a year since we've spoken. Even though it was about the logistics of our bank accounts, it ended in tears. His.

"Hi," I say, surprised, when he answers. When he says nothing, I say, "I saw the news. I just... I hoped you were okay."

"Here I am. Okay."

"I'm glad," I say. Then, "How are you?"

On weekdays, we would take the train into Manhattan together. I got off several stops after he did. The museum where I worked owned more art than we could ever display. Here, I know every coach by heart. Alone on the subway, I would gaze into my phone. Natural disasters, press conferences, Twitter jokes, advertisements—crolling past each with the pad of my thumb, photo after video after photo, on and on, forever.

In those days I bought salads that came in rigid plastic containers, which I ate with plastic forks—plastic that, still, years later, has not been absorbed by the earth. The meals I've long forgotten, but the forks remain in their landfill, where they'll linger for a thousand years. There was a photo I've never forgotten: a riverbank in Thailand, during the rainy season, heaped with plastic bottles like strange shells, mounds so high you couldn't see the sand. A child laughing amid the colorful plastic. It struck me as so beautiful, and so sad. What is it about the world, that it always feels like it's ending?

"I'm better, by the way," he adds. "I'm much better now."

"I'm glad."

We are alive at a time when two people can be miles away, yet in contact—voices disembodied and carried so I hear Jeff's voice directly inside my ears, as though it's inside my own head. No more days-long journeys in inclement weather, pulled along by weary horses.

I put on my red shoes and immediately the repaired heel gives out. The glue wasn't strong enough, or maybe I should have waited longer for it to set. In the hallway mirror I catch my own reflection: purple crescents beneath my eyes, hair charged like I've touched a balloon. My cheek is wet. Every day of my life, I wish I knew what to do.

GOOD SPIRITS

A ghost or a tiger. One would follow you for the rest of your life. Which one? Cecilia asked me again before she left for Johor Bahru—curious if I'd changed my mind. She chose ghost and I chose tiger. I always choose tiger. A ghost can't kill you, she said. But my reasoning has always been that a tiger doesn't mess with you, psychologically. They aren't devious like ghosts. Sure, a tiger might devour a limb. But a ghost could persuade you to cut off your own limb. Which is worse? To me it's obvious.

~~

The bus stops at kampongs and new villages, filling with girls like small fish in a trap. Speaking of small fish, Ma packs nasi lemak for lunch—extra ikan bilis because she is proud of me. Her youngest daughter, commuting to work! A real professional! Everyone's mothers had the same idea, and all of us carry banana leaf packets, little green purses. The bus deposits us, and we walk—a single herd—on the paved, smooth path to the brand-new building, then through an archway of pink and white balloons.

Cecilia's kampong used to be here. It was relocated—can you believe that? All the homes on stilts picked up like toys, moved elsewhere to make room for these towering silver buildings, this parking lot. When I close my eyes I can remember where each tree stood. You wonder why, when the announcement came that they were hiring, I said, *Sign me up*? Well, I have my reasons. First, I don't want to work with Ba at the herb shop. Second, Ma wants to marry me off to the second-eldest Chew boy, who isn't handsome like his brother and is constantly scratching the crotch of his shorts. Ma says the Chews are a "good" family. But I don't want him anywhere near me. It is 1982 and no one can tell me who to marry—or to marry at all. Third, since Cecilia went away, there is no one left who understands me. She works in a factory, too. In a letter she said, *There's peace and quiet. I'm finally living my own life.* I wanted to see for myself.

Inside, the machines make their own city. Even breathing here gives me pause, like my exhales are dirty and will leave marks like measles on the white walls.

We arrange ourselves into rows, as orderly as we can manage. A tall, light man introduces himself as our supervisor, Mr. Leeds. His eyebrows—and eyelashes, too—are clear like spiderwebs. When he speaks it is with an accent, like the queen's. Every third word, I don't understand.

Around me, the other uncomprehending faces belong to girls. Our dresses and headscarves flutter in the air-con. We will be making rubber gloves. Cecilia's factory makes microchips.

Our uniforms are sky-blue shirts with collars, along with hairnets and face masks. The scent of the locker room overwhelms with the prickly heat powder everyone has patted inside our armpits, me included. Too considerate of the others, trying to mask our scent, we have done the opposite, and made the atmosphere unbearable.

The clothing change transforms us strangers into a unit. At the assembly line, we line up even straighter. Mr. Leeds puts his key into a machine and flicks a switch. The machine groans, then begins to move: hands, all in a row, proceed mechanically forward, like soldiers. They bow and twirl. He laughs when we gasp. Can you blame us? It is nothing we've ever seen before. A belt moves the hands, and each hand dips itself into one substance, then another. At the end of the line, he removes a glove from the mold. He passes the finished glove around, and we take turns trying it on. How remarkable, that this was once the same rubber that dripped from a tree. It has been transformed into the oddest fruit.

My station will be near the end of the line: inflating the finished gloves to check for holes. I'm to entwine my fingers with the inflated gloves and squeeze to confirm that they're acceptable. Testing integrity, I plan to tell Cecilia, proudly.

We take our positions. The hands move forward. The factory floor is silent, but for the machine's gears turning. No one else speaks, we are so focused on our tasks.

"I'm Amina," whispers the girl who works beside me.

"I'm Melati," I whisper back, because I don't want to be Lai Ping here. Melati is the name Cecilia calls me.

I hold a glove to the spout. The air escapes from the sides and the hand won't inflate. It's challenging, getting it just right.

This is Monday. The first attack occurs Friday.

It takes only a few days to become an expert. The gloves I've inflated must number into the thousands. I'm bored. While working, my mind wanders to what I hope my mother will cook for dinner. I hope kangkung belacan. I'm teased for how much I love vegetables. It's why my family calls me "Little Rabbit."

We can hear Mr. Leeds singing to himself in the WC—his own private toilet because there are no other men here. It's a song about a tiger.

"I like this song," Amina says, and hums along.

It's almost time for our lunch break, our only pause in the day, when we hear a loud gasp. We look up to locate the source. The Malay girl who monitors the coagulation tank is walking backward, shaking her head at no one. Then she begins to shriek, flailing her arms like limp noodles. Our supervisor emerges from the restroom to see what the commotion is.

"Aiyo!" says the Chinese girl who stands beside her on the line.

"Why she screaming one?" adds the Indian girl, clearly irritated.

But the screaming girl, to our horror, dips her own hand into the hot water vat. She howls when it burns. Her hand turns bright pink, like raw meat. The ordinarily quiet factory floor is suddenly deafening: the loud sound of the machine grinding to a halt; her screaming; our layered, panicked shouts.

Paramedics arrive. The girl is strapped to a stretcher. She disappears behind the ambulance doors. It is my first time seeing an ambulance, and we watch it speed away, flashing and wailing.

Back inside, we huddle together, trying to piece together what happened to the girl, whose name is Vivy. Esther, who stands behind her on the assembly line, describes the way Vivy froze.

"Like she saw a ghost," Esther says, shuddering.

When Esther touched Vivy on the shoulder, and asked what was wrong, she didn't respond. Esther heard Vivy whisper, "Leave me alone," and start muttering a prayer to Allah. A moment later she was screaming that she was being attacked by a spirit.

"Back to work," calls Mr. Leeds.

We return to our positions. It is an effort, to stop my hands from shaking.

Lim Goh, who works the cornstarch station, is Christian, converted by British missionaries. According to her, there are no spirits except the Holy Ghost. She just means there is only the one, and it's a good one, we don't have to worry about it doing bad things to us. The rest of us are Muslim and Hindu and Buddhist and Taoist, meaning some of us believe in hantu-hantu more than others.

I've never seen one, but Cecilia has. Only once, when we were girls, playing in the jungle between her kampong and my village. The head of a woman, dragging long hair and entrails like the cans tied to a car for a just-married couple. She was inconsolable because her baby died in childbirth. She died, herself, of grief. By the time I turned to look, the hantu had disappeared. Cecilia insisted she saw it, though, and I swore I believed her, in the way that you must agree with your best friend. Being so sad you became a ghost was completely logical, we decided. It made sense to us.

After the spirit attack, our output is worse. I find this latest batch is hole-ridden; none of the gloves will inflate. Like the others, I'm spooked, dreading which of us might be next.

"Maybe it was Vivy's ghost," I say to Amina, an attempt to reassure her. "Her personal ghost. And we have nothing to worry about."

She has stopped humming.

"No," says Amina, shaking her head. "This isn't good. If there's a hantu here, none of us is safe."

~~~

My paycheck is more money than my father has ever made working for Uncle Boon at the herb shop. He grunts at the number, annoyed to be outdone by his own daughter. My mother, on the other hand, is pleased for her girl to outearn her lao gong. She stirs extra condensed milk into my tea. Now we can buy a new wok, and shoes for Ah Yoke's baby, who will be walking soon.

"Careful," my mother says, when I tell her about Vivy. "Spirits not happy."

"They're not interested in me," I tell Ma.

At home, my duties are the same. Helping my mother prepare dinner, peeling ginger and pounding shallots with the mortar and pestle. Fetching water from the well and filtering it through sand. Ma doesn't ask what the factory is like, which I'm grateful for. I wouldn't know how to explain it.

My little nephew cries. I shake white pepper on my half-boiled eggs—I like it so peppery it makes my eyes water. Ba pours me coffee for the first time, which inflates me with some pride, because it means he considers me an adult.

I miss Cecilia, and wonder when my real life will begin.

~~~

On our only day off, Cecilia and I agree to meet at the mall between her apartment and my workplace. The mall is crowded with people seeking refuge from the punishing heat in the free air-con. I spot Cecilia by the fountain and break into a run. We grasp each other tightly. It's been months since I've seen her.

"Let me go, lah," she laughs.

"You look different!" I say. "Why?"

Cecilia loosens her headscarf to show me a bit of her hair, which is permed, big and curly like a fern.

"Wow!"

"Shh," she says. "You can't tell anyone."

Women our age are heading into a store called Fresh Fit Pakaian. Making our way, we swap stories about our jobs. Her supervisor is from Taiwan. He's handsome and wealthy and wears a gold pinky ring with his own initial on it. The rumor is he is having a forbidden affair with a Malay girl. It's very scandalous.

I don't admit that my job is so boring. For some reason I don't tell her about the spirit attack, either.

"You'll be sick of it soon," she says. "Factory work—it's all the same."

"Never," I lie. I clasp her hands in mine, willing her to

be as delighted as I am. "Can you believe we're here? On our own?"

Cecilia nods. But in a distracted way, like she has something else on her mind.

"Maybe I could get a job at your factory? So we could be coworkers. And we could see each other all the time."

"You don't want to work with me," Cecilia says. "You're lucky. At least gloves are big. The microchips hurt my eyes. I think I'm going blind."

I hold up a green blouse that would be perfect on her.

"What about this one?"

"No, it's not for me."

"Just try it."

"I don't want to shop."

She folds her arms across her chest.

"This is a mall, lah," I say. "Jolli duit! Money is to spend."

I'm irritated with her, though I don't want to be. We don't have much time together.

I try a dress on myself—bright red like chili padi, a color I've never worn. I admire my reflection in the dressing room mirror. I open the door for Cecilia to see. It's sleeveless, and stops at my calf. My mother would shake her head: too revealing.

"It suits you," Cecilia says.

~~~

The next week, it happens again. To Esther this time. Mr. Leeds rushes into the women's restroom and emerges holding Esther by the armpits, dragging her out as though from a burning building. Her arms are wild and she is crying, screaming, "No no no no no!" Four of us have to pin her arms down. Lim Goh phones the paramedics.

Bintang whispers that flushing the toilet awakens the spirits. One of them lives in the toilet tank. The WC grows filthy because no one wants to risk disturbing the hantu.

"If they live in water," I say, "what about here?"

I point to the washing station, where Bintang supervises the washing of the molds, first with soap, then bleach.

"Don't say that," she says, shaking her head.

"You," Mr. Leeds says. Pointing to me. "You'll do Esther's job."

Then he points to Amina. "You stand here." He indicates the position at the coagulation tank where Vivy once stood.

My eyes meet Amina's fearful ones. He wants us to stand in the haunted places.

~~~

A bright pink rash appears on both of my hands. It grows redder when I scratch it. It's as itchy as two hundred mosquito bites. At home my mother rubs it with aloe vera, but it gives me no relief. The rash only grows angrier, covering my hands and creeping to my forearms in a dark jagged pattern.

Is it a spirit attack? I'm worried, picturing tiny tormented spirits, embedded beneath my skin.

"Could be," Amina says, when I show her my arms.

Emerging from the WC, Lim Goh swears that the wings on her menstrual pad flapped like a bird.

"I thought you didn't believe in anything but the Holy Spirit." Bintang smirks.

"Don't be mean, Bintang," Amina says.

"What do we do?" Lim Goh wails.

"If you smell frangipani, it means a spirit is close," Bintang says. "Ignore it. Just keep moving."

"Ladies." Mr. Leeds summons us for a meeting. "This is disappointing. I'm extremely disappointed. We have not met our quota."

Bintang raises her hand, meekly.

"Yes? You?" Mr. Leeds says. After three weeks, he still doesn't know our names.

"We cannot work, sir," Bintang says. "There are unhappy spirits here."

We murmur our agreement.

Mr. Leeds shakes his head in disbelief. It's as though we can see him thinking behind his clear eyes.

"I could fire you all," he says, raising his voice to be threatening. "Who of you believes in these . . . hantu-hantu?"

I don't need to look around to know that every last one of us raises her hand.

~~~

At the mall, I don't tell Cecilia about the spirits. I don't tell her that every day, I fear being possessed. If I admit anything is the matter, she'll think I'm not cut out for the factory life—like I'm a simple-minded person who belongs in a village. But that's not true.

"I want to get my ears pierced," I say instead.

At the discount jewelry store, I choose the smallest earrings, pretend diamonds, hoping my mother won't notice. Cecilia gets a second set of holes above her first.

After our piercings, we dabao our dinner, char kway teow. I follow Cecilia home. I'm staying with her for the weekend. Cecilia shows me around her apartment, cramped but remarkable to me, because she's chosen everything herself. Her lamp that needs to be jiggled to come on. Her dog-eared comic books. A small bar of soap that's shaped like a butterfly and smells like coconut—she chose that. I turn on her tap, and water streams out, her own private river.

One day I will be able to afford my own apartment, like Cecilia. It will be brand-new like the factory, with air-con and a toilet. My own sink, with running water! I can't imagine it. I feel sorry for my mother, who will have to fetch well water for herself. But not sorry enough that I will stay at home with her until I'm old.

"This is paradise," I say, falling backward onto Cecilia's bed.

I'm wearing my new red dress. I love how it looks, even though I would never wear it in public.

"Melati," Cecilia says, very seriously. "I have to tell you something."

I sit up.

"What is it?"

She presses her dress against her midsection, which looks larger than usual. Could she be—?

"Six months along," Cecilia says, confirming.

I'm not proud this is my first reaction, but I'm hurt. She's kept this a secret from me? All this time? I count backward. She was four months pregnant the last time I saw her. She is my closest friend. I would have told her if there was even a possibility of becoming pregnant. I try to wipe the hurt from my face and voice.

"How?"

"Never mind how."

"But who is the father?"

"Melati, don't ask me, lah! If you're my true friend you'll stop asking."

I open my mouth to ask another question, and close it.

"What will you do?" I ask, instead.

"I don't know," she says. "Me, become a mother? Can you imagine?"

She takes off her headscarf. She had to stop perming her hair, for the baby, so now it's half straight and half curly.

She joins me on the bed, and we lie back.

"Can I touch it?"

She moves my hand to her belly, which is taut like a balloon, yet harder than an inflated glove. We say nothing for a long moment. I wonder if Cecilia picks up on the battle in my mind, which is between hurt for myself, and joy for her.

"Remember the rambutan tree?" Cecilia asks. Her voice is dreamy.

"Of course."

"I wish I could just reach out my window and pluck a rambutan right now. The fruit was so sweet."

"It was. Those trees are gone now."

"It's sad, isn't it?" Cecilia says.

"I guess it's sad," I say, and shrug. "How do we know? It's progress. Progress means the future. The future is better than the past. That's how it's supposed to be."

"Chinese girls like you . . ." she begins.

"Chinese girls like me . . . what?"

She always calls me Chinese, even though I am not all Chinese. My grandfather is Orang Asli. But it's simpler to say.

"Never mind."

It's important that I am married off to a respectable family, because our family isn't entirely respectable.

At night, in bed beside Cecilia, I feel her baby kick against my back, like it wants me out of the bed. When I urinate in the night I don't flush. I don't want to wake her, but also I'm unsure if a spirit lives in her toilet, and don't want to risk a haunting.

I'm asleep when Cecilia begins to stir beside me. She mutters something.

"Cecilia, what's wrong?"

But she's still asleep, and doesn't respond. Her words grow louder, but remain incomprehensible.

Is it a spirit attack? Or is it only sleep talking, which my mother would say is the same? Cecilia begins to cry. She is still asleep, but she's crying, and I don't know what to do. I reach for her hand. Like me, she has a soul that is thumb-size. I hope my soul is inside my thumb right now and Cecilia's is inside hers. I take my friend's hand, and fall asleep holding it.

Lim Goh comes to work with a sachet of mugwort pinned to her breast. Others carry carved talismans in the front pockets of their uniforms; I can make out their outlines. I hope the spirit doesn't recognize me because my name is different. No one here knows my old name.

If every spirit used to be someone, who did the factory's ghosts used to be? I wonder if they're inhabitants of the cut-down trees, now loose because they're homeless.

A rumor begins: perhaps it's the spirits of those who died from a disease. Don't you know the reason we are making so many gloves? Lim Goh asks. The demand for medical gloves is because there is an epidemic. Do you know what AIDS is? The missionaries told her about it. You get it by being sinful. Be virtuous, and you will be okay.

~~~

At home my mother waits with an expression she wears when I have been naughty. It's a look that precedes her asking my father to take out the bamboo cane. But I'm too old to be caned, and I'm too old to be called Little Rabbit. My mother uses my given name, sternly.

"Cecilia... she isn't a good influence. I spoke to her mother. Even her mother agrees."

"What?"

"She is mixed up in bad things out there on her own—she's too modern. City girls, they become so liberated. It's dangerous! You come home straight after work. You can't see Cecilia anymore."

"But, Ma. It's not like that."

"Don't argue with your mother."

"She's the same as she always was."

"She's not." Ma eyes my shopping bag. A little bit of the red dress pokes out of the side. "And you're not the same, either."

~~~

Mr. Leeds is beaming with pride. Beside him stands a robed man, a bomoh. A shaman who will commune with the spirits and cleanse the factory floor. He is old and brown, so shriveled he resembles a child. He moves very slowly, removing what he needs from his plastic bag, which has a Fresh Fit Pakaian logo on it. He drops to the floor to pray. He sprinkles flour in erratic little piles on the floor.

"Over here," I say to him. "This area especially." I gesture to where Amina and I stand.

Afterward, over a feast of curry chicken, the girls chatter excitedly, appeased. I notice Amina isn't eating.

"He's a sham," Amina says, shaking her head. "He's not a real bomoh."

"How can you tell?"

"I just can."

I'm not sure what to believe. For a day, the girls work happily. Which only means that when it happens again, everyone but Amina is caught off guard. It's Lim Goh this time. The Christian! She drops to the floor and writhes like an overturned beetle, legs in the air.

"Not again," Mr. Leeds groans.

~~~

Somehow, past the heavy glass doors, a dragonfly is inside, and the machines must be paused, otherwise it will land in a vat. Mr. Leeds is frightened of its metallic eyes. The way he reacts to the insect, it's like he's seen a ghost, even though we know it's harmless. We spend the afternoon trying to net it. We're village girls. All of us have caught dragonflies before. We know how to catch them by their long bodies, these humming hairpins. But halfheartedly, here, we swipe nets in the air. A silent agreement not to catch it too quickly. It's a break from work, after all.

When Bintang appears on Monday with pink nail polish, Amina shakes her head. Spirits, she explains, can live in those chemicals.

"There could be hantu-hantu in your earrings," Amina says to me. "You have to be careful. You don't know where those gems came from."

~~~

"You're not seeing Cecilia, are you?" my mother asks.

I've packed my weekend bag. I tell her I'm staying with Cousin Loy, and my ma agrees, that's fine. Loy is boring, a good influence. My mother wants me to have a life as boring as Loy's, as boring as the Chews'.

I try not to seem surprised when Cecilia opens the door to her apartment. She is thin and pale and her face is covered in spots.

"Where are your earrings?" Cecilia asks.

"I thought they might be haunted."

She seems disappointed, so I put them back on, even though they turn my ears a bright red. I imagine a tiny, angry ghost in each lobe.

Cecilia says nothing about her own appearance. Her face looks as though it's been splashed with hot oil. Aren't we friends? I want to ask. Why won't you tell me what's happened? But I know I can't. She's told me not to ask questions. Her energy is dimmed, a fire reduced to embers.

That night I dream about birds. All the birds from our childhood, together in the jungle, sitting perched in trees. We're watching them do their strange bird activities, jerking their heads. And then it strikes me that we are birds, too, our chests feathered and puffy. Our flock begins to depart, flying into the sky, and we have no choice but to follow.

I feel a warmth and wetness in the bed. How shameful—have I wet myself? I turn on the light. Cecilia is still asleep, in a circle of blood, like a prayer mat.

At the hospital, the doctor comes to tell us that the baby is gone. Then he takes me into the hallway, and asks, "Are you her family?"

"Yes," I say.

He tells me Cecilia is sick, very sick. She should have seen a doctor earlier. They have medicine to give her, but it isn't a cure. Cecilia may not have very long to live.

"That's not right," I say to him. "We're only twenty."

"I'm so sorry."

When we return to the room, Cecilia is alert again.

"Can I see the baby?" she asks.

The doctor shakes his head.

"Please," Cecilia says.

At last, they bring her a small bundle. A little girl, gray green, like a lizard shedding its skin. A small, perfect nose. It's unpleasant to look at the baby, so I turn my attention to Cecilia instead, the love in her expression. I know, I just know, she would have been a wonderful mother.

"Don't look at me like that," Cecilia says. "Stop crying. Don't pity me. Don't."

Her parents have been called but refuse to visit. They are angry with her for becoming pregnant. And now they are angry with her for dying.

To Muslims, melati, the jasmine flower, means good health. It means healing. I am not Muslim, but I want to believe that, if I hold my friend long enough, I might be able to make her whole.

～～～

It seems wrong that I have to go to work in the morning. Glove after glove after glove, what is the point? Which of us will fall, next, to the ground?

"Where are you going?" Amina asks.

I walk to the WC. I've been holding my urine for two hours. It's there that I see her.

Who led her to the factory? Did she follow me here? Floating above the toilet is a familiar face, with its tiny nose, Cecilia's gray-green girl. Though I didn't look long, I recognize her.

"Hello," I manage.

She doesn't have anything to say to me—she doesn't know how to speak—but somehow I know this is her: Cecilia's baby, here to meet me.

She watches while I empty my bladder. Maybe she'll befriend the swamp spirit who lives in the toilet. The thought is pleasing to me.

～～～

At the hospital, I ask Cecilia, What if we could go back in time, to when we were girls?

We met when we were thirteen, in secondary school. We were fast friends, even though her family was Malay and mine mostly Chinese. She came to my house for Lunar New

Year and I went to hers for Hari Raya Haji. Our mothers joked that they had adopted daughters.

Would we be able to change something about back then? Cecilia asks. Or is it just that we would do it all over again?

I'm not sure. Which would you prefer?

~~

Let's say we don't change a thing. We are thirteen years old. Thirteen was younger then than it is now, older at the same time. We were still girls, but in a matter of years, we might be married. It seems impossible that we will ever be adults, with their creased brown skin and their yellowed eyes and their impatience.

It is bright and hot; the sky blue, the air heavy and wet. We stomp in the river until we feel the clay between our toes, and pull it out, a rusty red clump. We fashion the clay into vessels for ourselves: a saucer, a cup, a bowl full of river water. We buy assam laksa from our classmate whose mother makes it, who cycles from house to house, noodles balanced on one side and soup on the other. We eat it in secret. Our mothers will be angry with us; they don't like us to spoil our appetites. We visit the caves to cool down in the unbearable afternoons and shout until the bats fly around, in protest.

Cecilia asks me the question about ghosts and tigers. We are always asking questions, wanting to know the other's answers. Would you rather have only noses or only ears? Would you rather smell constantly like fish or like durian? There is a tiger that visits our village, though sightings are rare. I've never seen it. Auntie Sok claimed she saw one and it purred, though we know she is full of berak. My grandfather said that tigers and lions could roar but not purr, and smaller cats, like the ones kept as mousers in the village, purr but cannot roar.

It's an afternoon in spring, and we are sitting in the rambutan tree, eating the fruit and dropping the peels and pits to the ground, when we hear a man say, "Ow!" Beneath us are two businessmen. One is Asian, the other white. The Asian man isn't Chinese, he's lighter—Japanese. They wear suits and ties despite the heat, as though they might come across someone they might need to impress. They catch sight of us in the tree. Their relief is apparent that we are girls and not menacing creatures. The Japanese man gives us a wave. They have gifts for us: wrapped chocolate bars, melting in the heat, oozing from their foil. We eat them quickly, but the chocolate still coats our fingers, like mud but sweet.

"Do you like it here?" the white man asks.

We give them a tour, excitedly, Cecilia and I in a contest—who can impress them most. The clay in the river. The caterpillars sleeping curled in the banana leaves. We show them how to peel rambutans, which they've never seen before. Tasting the fruit, their eyes light up. To us, the rambutans don't taste sweet after the chocolate.

The change comes slowly, at first. Then it's enormous. The land is sold. In the years to come the trees are cut down, new buildings erected. Where do the gibbons and the birds and the civets go? Cecilia's kampong is moved and my new village remains, but the moment I leave, our homes will be torn down, too. Nothing to do, my ma says. Yet I can't shake the feeling that it's our fault.

~~~

Say it had all gone differently. We are thirteen. We are sitting in the rambutan tree when the mourning ghost joins us. Her name is Maryam. In this version of events, I see her, too, and she enjoys our company. Though she can't locate her own daughter, we will do. We pretend she is our mother, and Cecilia and I are sisters. Her intestines dangle from the rambutan tree, looking fine and shiny.

On the afternoon the businessmen appear beneath our tree, they cast their eyes up. We're a bizarre trio: a Malay girl, a Chinese girl, a ghost. Maryam flashes her creepy grin—her mouth of sharp white teeth. The men rub their eyes, unsure of what they're seeing.

Maryam makes a motion with her hands, a gesture you might use to say, *Look at this.* And at that, the leaves in the trees surrounding us rustle. One after another, the spirits emerge: the hantu tetek who smothers men with her tremendous breasts; hairy monsters who used to be men, women, and children who were murdered by the Japanese; the ghosts who live in the banana tree.

The businessmen cry out in fear. They drop their brown suitcases. They run. Powerful people don't always know the difference between someone who is scary and someone who has been wronged. We open up their abandoned cases. They're filled with papers: blueprints and contracts bearing tiny print. And chocolate bars—bribes for children. We are happy with our rambutans.

They never take the land, never excavate it, build onto it, never disrupt the wading birds or Komodo dragons. Or the spirits.

Word travels. Businessmen everywhere are spooked. The land is never developed, factories never erected. The storks never leave, storks with necks like the cane handles my grandfather carves from tamarind wood, when his hands cooperate.

Cecilia's kampong doesn't vanish. She never leaves home to work in the microchip factory and I never leave to work on rubber gloves. Cecilia doesn't become pregnant for the reason she won't tell me. She doesn't scream from nightmares, or water her pillow with tears. The spirits don't attack us because they have other concerns: preoccupied with their own dramas, as we are with ours.

For the rest of my life the tiger trails me, but I don't mind it. In fact, I grow accustomed to the company. Having an unknowable beast for a shadow means I never forget what is true, that I am always only seconds away from the whim that ends me, that it is a miracle and a mercy that I am here at all.

COLORS FROM ELSEWHERE

The wand was in her vagina. She had a vagina. She had hands, legs, lungs, a face with features that changed depending on her emotional state. A womb, containing an embryo she had been gestating for nine weeks and four days. Her husband, a regular man, stood at her side. The image of her uterus appeared on the screen, black, white, and grainy, like footage from the moon. And there, inside it, was the baby—though they weren't calling it a baby yet—in a position as though lying in a hammock, a spectral reverse silhouette. It reminded her of Casper the Friendly Ghost, a cartoon she'd watched as a child. She had been a child.

"If I'm silent," the doctor said. "It doesn't mean anything's wrong."

Silently the doctor moved the wand inside her. Silence didn't mean anything was wrong, but she thought to herself, silently, that something *did* seem wrong.

A minute later the doctor confirmed it. Not only was something wrong, the most wrong thing had happened: the baby's heart had stopped beating.

"Normally there is a flicker here..." The doctor pointed to the screen. The lack of motion was obvious.

The baby itself had stopped growing at some point in the last week. The baby was supposed to be the size of a cherry, but had stalled at raspberry. They hadn't yet called it a baby, though everyone else seemed so blithely willing to. And in a single swift instant, the title of baby was revoked. Instead of a baby, it was now the "products of conception."

On the drive home she wept—tears that were no different from yours or mine.

~~~

It surprised her, that there seemed to be no end to how much she could cry. She was accustomed to tears resulting in a cleansed sensation afterward. But now she cried for hours, without relief.

Friends sent flowers, soup, DoorDash gift cards. "It's so common," several friends said. The phrase was meant to be comforting, she knew, but the words landed in the opposite way. She didn't want to be reminded of how common it was. She wanted to wallow in the belief that what she was experiencing had never happened to anyone else. "You'll be pregnant again," other friends said. This, too, she couldn't believe. Unlike wine, fertility was not improved by age. The miscarriage seemed to confirm a belief she'd long held: that she was defective. Why couldn't her body do what other bodies did naturally? The majority of pregnancies succeeded. Why hadn't hers?

She lay in the fetal position. She watched episodes of *Monk*. She was angry when Sharona was replaced by bland Natalie. Her pain, though dulled by the medication she'd been prescribed, was still substantial. Her husband held her hand through the waves of it. He was supportive, practically and emotionally, but there existed a chasm between what he could understand and what she felt.

Though she had mightily resisted imagining the future while pregnant, she had. It was impossible not to. Pregnancy itself was a phase between one state and another: a temporary condition that promised you an entire human being at its conclusion. She'd compulsively checked the pregnancy apps—plural—she'd downloaded. They told her how far along she was, what to expect. Veiny breasts, morning sickness that could strike at any time of day, food aversions. Now she wished for an app that could tell her why this had happened. The doctor had said that 90 percent of miscarriages occurred because of chromosomal abnormalities. Most likely, there had been a fundamental incompatibility with life.

"What about the other ten percent?" she asked.

"One of every five pregnancies ends in miscarriage," her doctor only said.

Miscarriages were common, but having a miscarriage meant you were still the minority. It was tiring, always being in the minority.

Each day she cried a little bit less. On the first day, it had felt like she'd been hit by a bus, but with each passing day the vehicles grew smaller. On the second day, it was an RV. By the eleventh day, she felt like she'd been hit by a bicycle. It still hurt, but she felt less destroyed. She wished for the process to be over. She hoped at one point the grief would feel like nothing at all, like being hit by something as slight as a moth. She hoped for that at the same time she clung to grief itself, which radiated an assuring clarity.

At her follow-up appointment, the doctor showed her her empty uterus. The tenant had vacated—had left for someplace better, she couldn't help but think. Oblivion was better than being inside her.

"Any other questions?" the doctor asked.

Her discharge had seemed strange. She figured it was the result of putting eight pills in her vagina to expel the products of conception. The color of the fluid she produced had been shocking: green one day, purple the next, cycling through all the colors of the rainbow.

"My discharge is yellow," she said, which was true: it was yellow at the moment. She didn't mention that, last night, it had been aquamarine. The first four pages of Google held no answers.

She put her feet into stirrups and the medical assistant produced a speculum. While the doctor took a sample, she considered her next orders of business. Normally, she enjoyed making lists. Pregnancy had stripped her of her sense of control, but here she was, not pregnant again. The to-do list began to write itself in her mind. She would find an acupuncturist. She would go to the Korean spa for a full-body scrub—forcibly remove all the skin she'd had while pregnant. She would join a gym. She would eat all the things she hadn't been permitted: soft cheeses, cured meats, sushi. She would get drunk.

But she couldn't get drunk, not yet. She tested positive for a bacterial overgrowth that required antibiotics.

She went to pick up her prescription. The pharmacist asked, "Do you drink?" She was unsure of how to respond. She *hadn't* been drinking. She had been pregnant! In that moment of hesitation the pharmacist rushed to fill the silence: "Well, don't. I wouldn't drink for three, four days after you're done, either."

～

She wore loose-fitting clothing to her acupuncture appointment. Her Korean scrub would follow. After that she would call her local gym about a membership. The acupuncturist handed her a clipboard with a thick stack of forms she was to fill out. They were wholly unlike the intake forms she was used to from the regular doctor, forms that asked about her family history of diseases, whether she smoked, the date of her last period. These seemed to be screening for a complicated mission: they asked if she urinated in the night, if she often felt angry, if she had vivid dreams, if she had an aversion to wind. One of the forms featured a diagram of a human body and asked that she mark the areas where she felt any pain, and not only that, but also the quality of the pain: if it was stabbing, throbbing, burning, shooting, hot, or heavy.

"Nǐ huì shuō zhōngwén ma?" the acupuncturist asked. Do you speak Chinese?

She responded in English with the truth. She understood a little but couldn't speak.

The acupuncturist nodded. She placed her arm in a blood-pressure cuff. The sleeve tightened around her. People always looked at the number and declared it "normal." She didn't like the word *normal* in these situations. What she wanted was to be good. Her cholesterol was good. Her good cholesterol was good, her bad cholesterol was in a good range. When functions were measured and found to be *normal*, an involuntary panic rose inside her chest. *Could they be better?* she wondered.

She mentioned her miscarriage. She indicated lower and upper back pain.

"You're taking antibiotics?" the acupuncturist asked. There was a tinge of concern to her inquiry.

"For the infection," she said.

"Hmm." The acupuncturist frowned, as if she wanted to say more.

Silence didn't mean anything was wrong, she recalled. But she was tired of medical professionals—and now alternative medicine practitioners—not filling her in on the full story.

"What is it?"

"Try to relax. Lie down here."

She closed her eyes and let the needles enter her in various locations, regions selected for reasons unknown to her. They were areas she seldom thought of: the webbing between her index finger and thumb, her abdomen, near her foot. A warm, infrared light was placed above her feet so she wouldn't be cold. Flute music played, softly. She was given a button to press if at any point she grew uncomfortable.

She closed her eyes. During massages, she was often admonished to relax. She had never been sure what relaxation felt like, exactly. Had she ever really experienced it, being relaxed? Her baseline state seemed to involve a certain amount of clenching.

"Describe to me your discharge," the acupuncturist asked.

"Well," she began. "It's colorful."

She mentioned the aquamarine, the yellow, the fuchsia. For some reason it was easier to do because the acupuncturist was Chinese, too. The acupuncturist reminded her of her mother. No conventional doctor had ever reminded her of her mother. She watched the acupuncturist's face carefully. It displayed no reaction. The acupuncturist wrote down notes in Chinese, and she took a surreptitious photo of the page.

"Don't eat spicy food," the acupuncturist said. "Avoid ice water. I'll see you next week."

Later, she ran the photograph through an online translator. "Colors from elsewhere. An uncommon heart." She wondered what it could mean.

She finished the antibiotics. She waited the four recommended days, then got obliteratingly drunk. She ate sashimi, mortadella, camembert in sickening quantities. She told herself to enjoy the foods but, if she was honest, she went about the bingeing joylessly. When she bought berries at the grocery store, she bought the cheaper, nonorganic ones because it was only her, now. No one else.

Every raspberry saddened her a little. She had to remind herself that raspberries had reached their full potential; a raspberry would never grow into a cherry's size. Their embryo had been a raspberry, and that was all. It would never become a pumpkin.

Her discharge was mostly running clear again. There was only the faintest tinge of blue when she squinted.

Returning to the acupuncture clinic, she noticed it was bedecked in lucky bamboo. She'd been too fuzzed with grief the first time she visited, but she noticed it now. Bamboo tied with red ribbons, bundled like asparagus in glazed ceramic pots shaped like pandas and koi. Some bamboo spiraled up toward the ceiling. In one pot the spears were arranged in tiers, like a wedding cake. She noticed the water dispenser's red and blue spigots. There was tape over the blue spigot to warn against the cold water.

"What color is your discharge now?" the acupuncturist asked.

"Clear but with some blue."

"Let me see your tongue."

She opened her mouth. The acupuncturist murmured thoughtfully.

The acupuncturist moved her hair behind her ears.

"Oh! You have these."

She had small holes above both her ears—a birthmark, her parents had told her. Googling "holes above ears," she'd learned that the holes were called "preauricular pits." They were a congenital malformation—sinus tracts that weren't supposed to be there, proof of our evolutionary history as fish. Sometimes they oozed a putrid liquid. Not often, thankfully.

"Do they mean something? The holes?"

The acupuncturist said nothing at first. She rummaged in her file cabinet and extracted several sheets of paper. She flipped one of the pages.

"Will you tell me what you see here?"

It was the most elaborate inkblot she had ever seen, some kind of bizarre landscape.

"Is this upside down?"

"It's correct as is."

She described what she saw. What appeared to be trees sprouting from fluffy clouds. Planes in the sky that resembled fish. A sun like a child's drawing of a sun, but turned menacing—spikes protruding from it in a very punk rock manner.

The acupuncturist nodded. She held up a different sheet of paper. Another elaborate scene: this time the foliage was what looked to be the tops of pineapples. Curlicues—vines perhaps—framed the edges. What at first she thought were dancers—a man and woman in a waltz—were, upon closer inspection, possibly penguins. She described all this to the acupuncturist, who nodded.

"Have you ever felt . . ." the acupuncturist began. "Different? From other people?"

"Well, sure," she said. "Doesn't everyone?"

She remembered, as a child of six, lying in the bathtub, considering her small body. *I'm not like everyone else,* she'd thought to herself. But growing up disabused her of this belief. Year after year, she learned she wasn't unique. There were uncommon aspects about her, but they didn't make her exceptional.

"Is your uterus retroverted?"

"How did you know?"

The acupuncturist scratched a note onto her pad. It was one of those things—uncommon but normal. Her uterus tipped in a different direction from the majority of women's, back instead of forward.

"No ice water this week, either. I need to consult some sources. I'll see you next week."

Among her cohort it seemed that people vehemently did not want children, or vehemently did. It was more popular to stake out a position, to declare one's decision with utter certainty. Rarer were the people with her attitude, who were open to seeing what happened. She wondered if her ambivalence had caused the miscarriage. She *hadn't* desired a baby at all costs. Was that why she had lost it? Because she hadn't been fully committed, hadn't subjected herself to financially and physically punishing assisted reproductive technology to select the healthiest possible blastocyst?

From time to time she eavesdropped on trying-to-conceive forums, where users posted photograph after photograph of peed-upon sticks. Where there were abbreviations for everything, baby dances and two-week waits and days post-ovulation. She was sympathetic, but she wasn't one of them. And yet she had been disappointed, each month, when her period arrived. She had been thrilled when the pregnancy test finally read positive, first faintly, then more boldly. The ambivalence vanished and she was elated. How miraculous it all was. Her body was fashioning another body! She'd felt apprehension in addition to the joy, naturally, but she had been all in.

She went a day without crying, then two, then three. The swelling in her eyelids subsided, returning them to their regular size. She was beginning to feel like herself again—the way she had before she had become pregnant. Though this had been the goal, it troubled her. She didn't want to return to her previous state, exactly. It didn't seem right, that the experience had not left some kind of mark—no scar to reflect the depth of the pain she'd gone through.

At her next visit, she was surprised to find the acupuncturist, who normally wore plain scrubs and a hair covering, sporting her hair in large bouncy curls, and oval silver earrings, so long they nearly brushed her shoulders.

"I'm her sister," said the acupuncturist look-alike. She wore shocking pink lipstick. Her voice, though nearly identical, had more lightness in it. The acupuncturist appeared, in her typical uniform.

"We're twins. Though I'm a minute older."

"You can call us both Dr. Tang. I'm also a doctor."

At this, both Dr. Tangs laughed.

"She has a PhD in philosophy."

"Wow, okay. Hi. Nice to meet you, Dr. Tang."

"I thought my sister could be helpful."

"Oh! How so?"

"I'm not—I'm not so good with . . ."

"My sister can be too technical. All business. I'm here if you have any questions about your condition that are more . . . philosophical."

"What's wrong with me?" She began to panic. Was the sister Dr. Tang some kind of hospital chaplain, regretfully informing her that the reason for her infertility was that she was actually dying? And how had her doctor missed this? "Should I call my husband?"

"No, no," the acupuncturist rushed in. "What you tell him is your business. This concerns you and your . . . origins."

"What's wrong with me?" she repeated.

"You aren't from here."

"Sure, I know. I was born abroad but I was raised here."

"What we mean is . . ." the sister broke in.

She hesitated, so the acupuncturist continued.

"You aren't human."

"Excuse me?"

The philosopher elaborated. She was a human-adjacent life-form from a distant planet. She resembled a human, but was not.

But she had pain that responded to painkillers, she protested. Arms, hands, legs, lungs.

"Our lifespans are identical," the acupuncturist Dr. Tang said. "Our physical features, identical. Organs, nearly identical. Except in matters of reproduction. There are differences there."

"You won't be able to have children," the acupuncturist said.

"But I got pregnant."

"That can happen, sometimes. But such pregnancies never reach viability."

She felt dizzy. She reached for a rolling chair, which rolled away. Both doctors steadied it for her, and she sat. She regarded them. Was this an elaborate joke? It was January, not April. She grasped at her collar, fumbling to unbutton her top button. The acupuncturist began to fan her with a manila envelope.

"What's distinct about us can appear as normal human variation," the philosopher said. "What humans call 'tipped uteri' and 'preauricular pits,' for example, are uncommon here but a dominant trait on our home planet."

Us. Home planet. She looked from one sister to the other. "So you two . . . you aren't human?"

"We are not," said the philosopher sister.

"Is every . . ." she began. The question was absurd, but she had to know. "Is every Asian an alien?"

"Not at all, a very small percentage, in fact."

"What does that mean? Ten percent?"

"Much less. Point five percent, if that."

"Most aliens look Asian. The others look vaguely eastern European. But we don't prefer that word."

"What do you call yourselves?"

"We call ourselves the Acela."

"Like the high-speed train?"

"The train was actually named by one of us. A nod."

She pinched herself. It hurt.

"I hope we can assure you . . . your origin is of no major consequence. Reproduction is the primary area of divergence."

"In every other way you are practically indistinguishable from a human."

"But you're saying I can never have children."

"No."

"Sadly not."

"What if I found a male Acela to reproduce with . . . ?"

"The male Acela live on ^&*+%," the acupuncturist said, matter-of-factly, making a sound she had never heard before, pronouncing the name of her—their?—home planet.

"In our culture it is the females who are the explorers, who venture to distant lands. The males and other-gendered tend to the children and homesteads."

"How did I get here?"

"That, we cannot tell you. It's possible your mother voyaged while pregnant with you. On our planet gestation lasts decades, and begins as early as age ten. And memories form later. Infantile amnesia persists longer."

"She is pretty secretive about her past. But I thought that was an immigrant thing."

"It *is* an immigrant thing. We are immigrants, after all."

"It's also possible she doesn't know. Acela are sometimes sent as children and not told about their origins."

"Do you miss home?"

"These bamboo are antennae," the original Dr. Tang said, simply.

~~~

Dazed, she walked toward her car. The acupuncture office was next to a middle school's pickleball courts, which were separated from the sidewalk by a tall chain-link fence. A neon ball flew over and narrowly missed her skull.

"Ma'am, could you help us?" called a prepubescent voice. "Our ball?"

She didn't consider herself a ma'am, but supposed she was. She tossed the ball over.

Sliding into the driver's seat, she felt a creepy sensation in her skin. Eyes met hers from the bed of the truck parked directly in front of her. A deer's black eyes. She nearly shouted from fear. It was just the mounted neck and head, immense branching antlers. Taxidermy was something she had never understood about human beings. She texted a photo to her husband. He replied: "Is that real?" Everything was less shocking in a photo. She wished there were a way to send messages that communicated visceral experience.

The news was tremendous, life-altering. Of course it was. But a part of her felt relief. All her life, she'd believed herself different. Now she was justified in that suspicion. Here was a reason for her inability to carry out this basic human function of reproduction. She wasn't human.

Driving, she peered into the car windows of everyone around her. A young man drowsily nodding along to music. She could feel the bass in her own car, traveling up her legs. A mother chauffeuring chubby toddlers in two car seats. Certain car windows had been tinted so darkly she couldn't make out the drivers within. Was that legal? It reminded her of alien movies where the creature inside the spaceship was hidden behind dark alien glass. Her own windows were untinted, yet she supposed she was that creature.

This wasn't a Pinocchio situation. There wasn't a path to being human. She simply wasn't, and that was all.

She was two when her family immigrated to the United States. Her family had won the green card lottery. She remembered having her photograph taken for a laminated card that said RESIDENT ALIEN.

~~~

She called her mother.

"Hi, Mom," she said.

"Auntie Suzie gave me shoes, but they don't fit. I give them to you. Okay?"

"Sure. Mom, I have to ask you something. Does the word *Acela* mean anything to you?"

"Acela, Acela." A pause. "Is it a flower?"

"No."

"You mean the car?"

"What? No, not Acura, Mom. Never mind." This required a different tactic. "Can you tell me your earliest memory?"

"So many questions! I don't remember!"

"I'm not asking about what you don't remember! What's the first thing you *do* remember? From being a child?"

"Oh, I don't know. Playing with my sisters?"

Her mother had always been terrible with details. How

could she expect any different now? Either her mother was lying or she was unaware of her origins. She didn't push further. And if her mother didn't know? The detail of her heritage was relevant only to reproduction, so what did it matter? Years ago her mother had complained about hot flashes. Now she'd settled, happily, into postmenopause.

~

Her file cabinets contained countless bottles of prenatal vitamins and herbal supplements. She'd gotten rid of years of files and receipts to make space for them. An audit had felt abstract; infertility, immediate. Now she rubbed open a trash bag and filled it with the supplements. The bag rattled, a bizarre percussive instrument. She threw it away.

She and her husband ate dinner. They watched their show. She narrowed her eyes at each actor on the screen. Could that actress be Acela? Or that one? It was possible, but not especially likely.

~

The next morning, she returned to the acupuncture clinic. She didn't have an appointment, but did they expect her to just go about her day? The Tangs were rearranging furniture—bickering about the placement of one particularly towering bamboo plant.

"The feng shui is better this way."

"What do you think?" the philosopher asked.

"I like it where it is now."

"Did you get some rest?" her doctor asked.

"No."

The philosopher recognized her distress.

"You know, there are options. If you'd like to be among your people."

"*People*." The other Dr. Tang chuckled softly.

"The journey isn't short. But that's what cryosleep is for. We can tuck you in a sleep pod and you won't age a day."

The hair on her arms stood at attention. There were others like her. Perhaps on her home planet she wouldn't have to feel the way she did. Defective.

"What's it like? Over there?"

"Culturally, it will take some adjusting. Children are raised by the males, as we mentioned. The females are milked regularly and all milk goes into a communal vat. And that's just the child-rearing experience..."

"Clothing is optional, but we don't have the same types as we do here. We only have skirts."

"For all genders?"

"Yes. And we only have red."

"We don't really have music genres. The closest approximation would be... What do you think?" Dr. Tang turned to her sister.

"EDM is similar."

"All music is EDM?"

"More or less. That's the only way we can explain it that you might understand."

"The sunsets are to die for. Breathtaking."

"We have different suns."

"There's nothing like it here."

Instead of heading home, she sat by the reservoir. Earth's sun reflected brightly off the surface of the water, the only sun she'd ever known. She watched a duck attempt to drown another duck and looked around, wanting to cry for help. Troubling as it was, it was what ducks did.

Humans jogged, Rollerbladed, pushed strollers. There were human beings of all kinds on display.

On a nearby bench, a bald man with a middle finger tattooed on his cheek held a Popsicle that resembled Spider-Man. In his other arm he held a baby, also bald. Their likeness was obvious. The baby reached for the Popsicle and the man let it lick with its tiny pink tongue. It reminded her of a butterfly dipping a proboscis into a flower—the focus.

She found herself tearing up. She hadn't cried in weeks, but she didn't bother trying to stop herself. These tears weren't the overburdened kind. Crying like this was a harmless pastime.

"Excuse me." The tattooed man was beside her now. "Could you hold him for me? For a second? I really have to pee."

Perhaps he thought a crying woman could be trusted. She nodded. The man passed her the baby first, then the Popsicle.

"It's okay if he has some." The man ran toward the restroom.

The baby continued enjoying the Popsicle, fluttering, happy.

She had once been an infant, dependent and defenseless, swaddled and held and changed. She had graduated from kindergarten and high school and college. She had gone to the prom, not happily. Her father had taught her to drive, which had started out harrowing and now was second nature.

The baby was incredible at maintaining eye contact,

seldom blinking its large, glossy brown eyes. She wondered who the baby might one day become. Would he enjoy school? Would he go to prom, or would prom be a relic of the past? Would he learn to drive, or would there be something better than cars by then? She couldn't help but feel some kinship with him. They weren't both humans, but they were both beings.

There were very few truly universal experiences, if you thought about it. Now the phrase made her laugh. Of course, humans claimed "universal." What were the human experiences? Being born, and dying. Breathing, eating, defecating. Joy and grief weren't even necessarily universal. Alexithymia was a condition in which one did not feel emotion. There was not a single film or book that everyone agreed on. But here was the baby, feeling joy at a Popsicle, as she'd once felt joy at a Popsicle. One day he would most likely feel grief, as she had over her miscarriage, though not exactly in the same way. His strand of grief would be different from hers, but it was all part of the same fraying ribbon.

The baby made sweet grunting noises. Could she choose a planet she didn't know over this one she did? A hypothetical Acela child over the husband she loved? The prospect of being milked like a dairy cow, wearing a red skirt, while EDM played . . . none of it appealed. But maybe it made sense over there. Would she feel a belonging she'd never felt before? She could go to cryosleep and awake on a planet of alien foliage, where penguins danced to pulsing music in the air.

"Thanks," the baby's father said, taking the baby back. When he smiled, the finger on his cheek crinkled.

It was so large, his tattoo. She wondered if he regretted it or if he still found it funny. Getting a tattoo on your cheek meant not getting a different tattoo on your cheek. This made her feel some way she couldn't quite articulate yet. But it was a positive feeling.

Procreating was not a universal experience. It was merely a common one. All along, she'd been ambivalent, she reminded herself. Not everyone got to experience motherhood. She would be one of the people who didn't, and it was fine, she thought sadly but firmly. It was fine.

~~~

At home, her human husband stood at the sink with suds cupped in his hands, pink from the hot water.

"Are you okay?"

She wondered why he asked that, what sort of expression her face was holding. She wasn't always in control of it. He knew so many of her secrets. How would he take this one? She remembered the chasm she'd felt between them, during the active part of the miscarriage. For all his support, he couldn't fully relate to her experience. He didn't know what it was like to be her. She hadn't known then that she was a literal alien. Now the chasm made perfect sense.

"Hi," she said, and hugged him from behind.

Being married, like being pregnant or miscarrying or dying, was among the most common of activities. Yet it was always experienced singularly. Even if it had happened infinitely throughout history, the individual's experience could not be anything but monumental. She had gotten married because she loved him, in particular. She had loved him in particular and he had loved her in particular, and their two particular selves had formed a combination that had never existed before. Words had been used in all manner of ways, but it was still possible to write a new sentence. She thought of the baby in the park, wriggling day by day into specificity. His father flipping everyone the bird on a regular basis. The choices this baby would someday make, and what would be decided for him. All of that adding up to his life.

"I don't think it's happening for us," she finally said.

"The baby?"

"The baby. The family."

"We're already family."

"True."

"That's okay with me. We'll still have a good life. We already have a good life."

She liked hearing him say that. A good life, in the singular. She supposed they had their own lives, and then their marriage was its own third thing: a third life.

He wiped his hands on a dish towel. He gathered her close. The chasm was there but there was a tightrope over it.

A child would have been a fourth life, and then together, all together, they would have had a fifth life. She would have liked to multiply her life. She would have liked to meet that child. He would have been a good father, if only he had chosen someone—nearly anyone—else.

But now she felt the warmth of his body, the same body that had held her in her grief that winter. It was a warmth like hers, like yours or mine—the heat, not of being human, but of being warm-blooded, and alive. Her imagination traveled to the stars, past the planets she knew, and past the planets she didn't. Then it made its way home.

D DAY

And on the 2,556,750,000th day, God reconsidered what he had made, and decided the world would be better off if human beings were other animals entirely—if there were no such thing as human beings at all. There would be species, but there wouldn't be races. You wouldn't look at a fellow zebra's face and think yourself superior. You wouldn't amass untold wealth. You would murder, at times, but no one would take it personally. (In the absence of people, "personally" wouldn't be a thing.) You wouldn't buy a gun and shoot children. You wouldn't invent nuclear weapons. You wouldn't blithely burn fossil fuels and irreversibly affect the planet's climate.

Jade was at her best friend Ruby's house when both of their phones pinged with the news, like it was an Amber Alert or a hurricane warning. Ruby wouldn't have been surprised if God were the subject of an Amber Alert. Look out for God, driving a windowless white van. He probably had a vanity plate. To be honest, Ruby didn't think very much of God.

Jade was straining pasta over Ruby's sink. The hot steam

rose into her face, a carbohydrate facial. Ruby stirred the pot of sauce on the stove. A bubble popped and splashed red tomato not on her apron but just to the side of it, onto her white shirt. This was always happening to Ruby.

"What animals have friends?" Jade asked Ruby.

Ruby typed the question into her phone.

"Cetaceans are capable of true friendship," Ruby read. "Higher primates, elephants, camelids, certain members of the horse family."

"Camelids are camels?" Jade asked.

"And llamas and alpacas."

At the end of the month, God declared, all people would be transformed. Ruby, Jade, and the rest of humanity would have thirty days to select what they wanted to spend the rest of their lives as. They had the entire animal kingdom to choose from. After the deadline, humans would not exist.

They sat down to eat their dinner. Ruby poured wine into her favorite little glasses from the museum store, which were shaped like eggcups. The friends clinked their glasses together and drank.

"What animals get drunk?" Ruby asked.

"That one I know," Jade laughed. "Elephants and parrots. Deer, moose, bats."

"So elephants have friends *and* get drunk," Ruby mused.

"Except it takes a lot to get them drunk. Obviously. Females are . . ." Jade peered into her phone. "Six to eight thousand pounds."

"It would be nice, weighing six to eight thousand pounds and not obsessing over it."

Jade twirled spaghetti around her fork and conveyed it to her mouth.

"What'd you put in this sauce? It's so good."

"Fish sauce! You like it?"

"I'm going to miss your cooking."

"You won't, though," Ruby said, laughing sadly. "I mean, that's kind of the beautiful thing."

The change was meant to take us down a peg. A naval term. A ship's colors were maneuvered via pegs. There were higher and lower colors, more and less honorable ships. Humanity was to be taken down a peg so we would stop coming up with such stupid terms to begin with.

For the first two weeks after the announcement, political bickering paused. Instead, zoologists were in high demand, appearing on television shows, looking a bit confused by their newfound fame. Nature shows, which had been declining in popularity, saw a surge in viewership and revenue.

"What's your choice?" people asked one another. Everyone, everywhere was trying to make sense of things: ferret out the superior choice. (Not ferrets, or other rodents, for most.)

Ruby thought it was ludicrous. The point was to be freed of trivial human concerns, and yet humans were already trying to extrapolate based on human social conventions, like romance and marriage. Penguins were well publicized as animals that mated for life. Many, many people wanted to be penguins, but were we going to have a world full of penguins? When it was getting so warm? Mammals were most popular: cold-bloodedness left many, well, cold. It was the same with insects. God had declared extinct animals an option, but of course, it was possible, even probable, that you might go extinct again.

In the United States, the choices soon became political. Ruby thought this, too, was absurd: there was nothing inherently political about animals, but once the partisan pundits took sides, you could predict what an American would choose based on their political affiliation. Conservatives tended not to go with anything that underwent metamorphosis, like caterpillars or tadpoles. They were unwilling to become anything too radically different from themselves. As a result, they were primarily interested in primates, like orangutans and gibbons. Libertarians gravitated to lone wolves and fiddler crabs—every-"man"-for-"himself"-type animals. They liked defensive animals, too: porcupines and skunks.

Liberals were sensitive to the fact of climate change, and opted for animals that could withstand extreme heat and would do best in the sweltering climate of our near future. They thought of themselves as individuals, committed to creative expression, but really, when it came down to it, they wanted to do what celebrities did—what was trending on social media. They wanted to be part of a literal flock. Geese and sheep were popular choices.

There were unbelievers—staunch atheists and staunch conspiracy theorists. We hadn't seen God, had we? they argued. It was only an alert we got on our phones. How could we know for certain that that had been a message from God, and not some Russian scammers? They didn't believe the change would actually happen. And if God indeed materialized, needing to know what animal you'd like to be? The unbelievers planned to panic-order, like at a restaurant. Their blurted-out answer would reflect their truest desire.

~~~

Jade and Ruby met at their favorite old movie theater. It was painted with a large detailed mural dating back to 1922. Every time they examined it they found some element they'd never noticed before. Today it was a nude baby in the corner, casually holding a watermelon. At the concession stand, Jade ordered a large popcorn from an acne-riddled teen named Halvor.

"What's your choice?" Jade asked Halvor. It was small talk now.

"Electric eel," Halvor said.

"Very cool," Jade replied.

Ruby produced the friends' preferred condiments from her purse: furikake, sea salt, a double-bagged baby-food jar of melted butter.

They had been friends since they were six years old. That was thirty years of being friends. At six, they'd made "perfume" together by steeping rose petals in water; at twelve, they'd practiced freak dancing; at eighteen, they'd held the other's hair back as they puked from too many Jell-O shots. They knew which movie the other wanted to see without asking.

There had been a deluge of personal essays and podcasts about the impending change, which everyone was now calling "Devolution Day." D Day. It was such a human impulse, to call it a regression. But there hadn't been enough time for the medium of film to grapple with the concern of the day, so going to the movies was still a very anthropocentric activity.

This movie was about a pianist on a deserted island. He had to build his own piano using vines and pieces of his shipwrecked ship, with shells for the keys. All the native animals lived on this island without the torment that afflicted this shipwrecked man, but of course, the film was about the human who struggled against the elements and missed music so badly that he spent days processing coconuts into piano material.

The friends emerged from the darkened theater, their eyes squinting to adjust to the light. Ruby loved the movie. Her tastes were a little more expansive than Jade's were, because Ruby had seen more and stranger movies. Ruby could tell, from the neutral expression on Jade's face, that Jade hadn't liked the film, so she tempered her enthusiasm for it. Jade didn't fully express her dislike of it. But it wasn't a lack of honesty that kept them from sharing. They weren't the sorts of friends who had spirited exchanges over art. Ruby had those friends, friends who derived pleasure from aesthetic arguments. There was the pleasure of combat—articulating your differences in perception, insisting on your rightness. Though those conversations could be a lot of fun, you could leave the encounters feeling more rigid in who you were.

With Jade it was different, and Ruby thought it made their relationship more special. It did make Ruby a little sad, that she couldn't gush over how wonderful she'd found the movie. Ruby thought it had articulated something inarticulable, in the way transcendent art did. She felt emotionally pierced, changed. But although commonalities bolstered a friendship, Ruby knew better than to be hurt by Jade's lack of enthusiasm. It happened more frequently than you might expect, that someone you loved loved different things from you.

～

At their favorite pho restaurant, Jade ordered for both of them, their usual order. Two rare steak phos, two Vietnamese iced coffees, and a number forty-four, barbecue pork vermicelli, to share. Ruby squirted hoisin and sriracha into a little dish, in a yin-yang symbol.

"I quit my job," Jade said. She worked with a woman who made leather handbags. "It felt wrong."

"I thought they were vegan leather?"

"I mean, yeah. But still. The *concept* of leather, now." Jade shuddered.

Their pho arrived: pink lily pads of rare meat, thin rings of white onion.

"Animals that get the most sleep," Ruby said, "are sloths, koalas, bats, armadillos, cats."

"You know, bats sleep a lot *and* get drunk. So those are pluses. But they gross me out."

"You're only finding them gross because of your own humanness. You wouldn't find yourself gross as a bat. You wouldn't, like, consider yourself in any reflective surfaces."

They were both artists—Jade a painter and Ruby a novelist—but Ruby had always been the more practical of the two. It was what it was; Ruby disliked her practicality. Every day she wrote for four hours. She drank alcohol only on weekends. In her thirties, she metabolized it less efficiently, so any amount ruined her writing mornings. She lived by Flaubert: "Be boring and orderly in your life so that you may be violent and original in your work."

While everyone was busy being upset that they would be transformed into non–*Homo sapiens,* Ruby had come up with a spreadsheet of animals, listing the pros and cons of each.

"Don't make fun of me, but I'm thinking of seeing an astrologer," Jade admitted.

"Jade!" Ruby said, shocked.

"I knew I shouldn't mention it."

"No. I'm sorry. Of course you should. I'll be curious to hear what they think."

~

Even though there was less than a month left of capitalism itself, businesses sprang up. Consultants who claimed to be able to look into your soul, via your eyes, and tell you exactly what animal you were meant to be. Astrologers who could tell you, via your birth chart, what was best for you. It wasn't as straightforward as Leos being lions and Cancers being crabs, no, it was vastly more complicated than that, and depended on your ascendant, where your Neptune was placed, your midheaven.

Real estate developers pivoted from luxury condos to luxury holding pens and aquariums, as though any animal would elect to live in captivity, however luxurious. Ruby thought it was terrible and predatory and greedy.

Then there were the orgies. A nightly party sprang up on both coasts called "Last Gasp." But the frantic sex-having struck Ruby as absurd, too. Animals were having orgies constantly. Or was it unwanted sexual advances? It depended on the animal, Ruby supposed. Still, sex in the animal kingdom seemed, for many species, less fraught than human dating.

"What animals experience sexual pleasure?" Jade asked Ruby.

"Not cats. Razor penises." Ruby shuddered.

"Dolphins, maybe."

"Don't dolphins seem so, I don't know, basic? The golden retrievers of cetaceans."

"Definitely." Jade dipped a raw bean sprout in sriracha. "I've been thinking bonobo. Except that's what all the tech bros want to be."

"They won't be tech bros as bonobos, though. None of us will be anything."

"Yeah. But don't you think some tech bro essence will remain?"

"No, I don't."

"We should be together, though. Don't you think? I'm not seriously considering bonobo."

"Not as penguins. I refuse to be a penguin."

"We won't be penguins."

Jade's glasses were foggy. She wiped them with a microfiber square she carried in her purse.

"You know all those preppers who thought they should get LASIK because of the apocalypse?" Ruby mused. "Now it doesn't even matter. You could be an animal who sees *better* than humans. You could see more color."

"Which ones are those?"

"The mantis shrimp has sixteen color-receptive cones. As compared to our three."

"Butterflies probably have good vision."

"I wonder if God would let us be rocks," Ruby joked. "Jade and Ruby. Stay who we are, forever."

"There would be nobody around to find us precious. To wear us as adornment."

"There's something very lovely about that," Ruby agreed, happily.

~~

One week remained. Ruby wanted to bask in the most human things. What were they? To her they were domestic tasks that most others found unspectacular: cooking noodles, solving crossword puzzles, replacing the ink in her fountain pen. Pumicing her rough feet. Responding to emails with "Sorry for my delay in getting back to you." She even savored, for the first time, sitting in traffic on her way to Jade's apartment.

"What's the most human thing we could do right now?" Jade asked.

"Escape an escape room? Bake a multilayered cake?"

Jade nodded.

"Let's bake a cake and do an escape room."

They were frosting the cake when Jade, using the offset spatula to smooth the frosting around the cake's sides, spoke.

"I think I want to be a whale," Jade said.

She seemed nervous to be saying this out loud, and Ruby turned, surprised, to her friend. In her hand she held edible flowers harvested from Jade's container garden, and she felt her fist involuntarily closing around them, crushing their delicate petals. It had been three weeks since the announcement, but it was the first time either of them had expressed a real desire. Until that moment, they'd only brought up possibilities in a joking way.

"Oh, wow," Ruby said. She tried not to seem too shocked, or at all alarmed. "What kind?"

"Bowhead whales live to two hundred."

Ruby affixed the flowers—pansies and calendula—to the sides of the cake. It was a two-tiered carrot cake. Their hands were orange from grating the carrots.

"I don't know if I want to live that long," Ruby said, slowly.

"Really?" Jade asked. "Don't you think it would be fun, being in the same pod for two hundred years?"

"I would love to be in your pod," Ruby assured her. "I think they're also called gams."

"What if we chose a shorter-lived whale? Blue whales only live to eighty or ninety." Jade's voice had a tinge of desperation in it. "Or beluga whales live to fifty. Plus, they're cute."

"We won't know that we're cute."

"Don't be like that, Ruby," Jade said. Tears were gathering in her eyes. "Be honest with me. Could you be a whale?"

"I don't know, Jade," Ruby said. "I have to think about it."

They sliced and ate the cake in silence. When it came time for their escape room appointment, Jade told Ruby she wasn't in the mood.

"Oh, okay," Ruby said. "We could do something else. We could grill a couple steaks? That's very human."

"Actually, I think I'd rather be alone right now," Jade said.

"Okay," Ruby said. "Of course. No problem."

She took her car keys from Jade's kitchen counter. She hugged her friend, who returned her embrace stiffly.

~

Her whole life, Ruby had felt like a weirdo. What other people had—groups of friends, romantic partners, weddings where they were treated like celebrities, spacious houses, adorable and well-behaved children, covetous experiences—Ruby had never wanted. She wasn't shirking these things as a point of identity, like a digital nomad or monk, but simply because she had always viewed them as extraneous—empty.

Only two things made her feel like she wasn't completely inhuman. One was working: immersing herself in her writing. The other was being around Jade. Writing didn't prove that she wasn't a waste of humanity. It was merely something she enjoyed and felt called to do. No one asked her to do it. In fact, most people found it bewildering that she kept at it. Everyone seemed puzzled that she was a writer, despite not being Ocean Vuong. I wish I were Ocean Vuong, too, she wanted to say to these people. Not because he was famous, but because he no longer had to justify his existence. It wasn't questioned, his compulsion to spend precious time—the last days—considering the placement of commas.

It was being around Jade, a human being, that made her feel like she wasn't wholly worthless. Ruby thought of how she had recently picked up what looked like a tiny black seed from her kitchen counter. Was it a seed, or bead, or piece of plastic? Viewing it under a magnifying glass, she saw that it had numerous tiny legs. One leg moved. She shrieked and dropped the bug somewhere on her kitchen floor.

Since then, she had thought of herself that way: a minuscule life-form, no larger than a sesame seed, that made God shudder a little in disgust. Only Jade had witnessed Ruby in every iteration of her life and not fled. They hadn't even vowed to stay together, as married people did. And yet Jade remained, and Ruby, too. That counted for something, didn't it?

Ruby loved her friend so dearly. Why couldn't she agree to be a whale? It could be so simple. And yet something held her back.

Thirty-two hours remained. Jade and Ruby carpooled to their friend Cassandra's house. In their larger friend circle, everyone had been throwing extravagant parties, trying to spend all the money they could before money no longer mattered. Last week, they'd attended a party with butter sculptures, and not one but four ice luges. Ruby received a chilled vodka shot from an ice penis chiseled with veins, originating from a glistening male torso. At another party, a turducken sat on an enormous doily. The host sliced neatly into it with an electric carving knife, exposing the wonders within, a breathtaking meat geode.

Cassandra welcomed them. She wore a silk dress that draped beautifully across her round, uniquely human breasts. Servers, hired from a pool of unbelievers, circulated with champagne flutes and crystal dishes of the finest beluga caviar. In the future, no one would really eat caviar except for bears, and maybe larger fish, though they wouldn't comprehend it for the delicacy that it was.

Jade and Ruby were pleased to see their friends enjoying themselves, but as usual, the two of them wound up talking to each other. Ruby's parents planned to be turtledoves, and her younger brother would be a partridge. They were irritated with her for not wanting to be a bird along with them. Ruby's mother was so bereft she wouldn't speak to her. But Ruby had always been the odd one out—the odd duck, so to speak.

Jade's mother wanted to be a poodle, even though Jade had encouraged her to pick something wilder. How would a domesticated dog manage without a human owner? Would it even know how to hunt? It would be better to be a house cat,

Jade had argued. But stubbornly, Jade's mother insisted on being a poodle.

"What are you thinking?" Jade asked finally. The friends had been avoiding the question all night, wanting to enjoy the party.

"I think," Ruby said, slowly, watching her friend's face. "I think I want to be a turtle."

Ruby always postponed decisions right up until the deadline. She had abandoned her spreadsheet. She always tried to plan things—it was this way with her writing, too—but in the end this, like writing, was an intuitive endeavor. She couldn't explain it, but Ruby felt, deep in her bones, that she wanted to be a turtle.

Jade loaded a potato chip with caviar, placed the entirety of it on her tongue, and chewed for a long moment.

"But turtles live even longer than whales," Jade said, as neutrally as she could manage.

Ruby saw that Jade's teeth were gray from the bite.

"I guess it wasn't about the lifespan at all," Ruby admitted. "I don't know if I can explain it."

"A freshwater turtle?"

"I don't think I want to be a sea turtle, unfortunately."

"So we won't even be in the same bodies of water."

"I know, Jade. I'm sorry. You can't let me hold you back from being a whale."

Jade said nothing.

"Please. Please don't be mad at me," Ruby said. "I couldn't stand it if you were mad at me in our last—" She looked at her watch. "Twenty-nine hours."

Jade said nothing, still.

"I'm just sad," Jade said, finally. "I'll miss you."

"You won't actually—"

"Stop it, Ruby," Jade said, angrily. "Don't tell me I won't be able to miss." Tears fell down her cheeks in two dramatic rivulets. "I *will* miss you."

"And I'll miss *you*, Jade," Ruby said. She'd told herself she wouldn't, but she started crying, too.

Jade slept over at Ruby's. In the morning, they indulged in a hungover feast of painkillers and waffles and bacon, which Ruby made extra crispy, the way Jade liked. Afterward, they climbed onto Ruby's roof and threw dirty dishes off the side of it, because they didn't need to wash them anymore. The dishes shattered satisfyingly on the asphalt.

In their final daylight hours they had plans to hang glide, scuba dive, and say goodbye to their families. The hang gliding and scuba diving were ways of confirming their choices. As a turtle Ruby would never know flight. And Jade needed to make sure the ocean was where she truly belonged.

The hang gliding was done in tandem. Ruby and Jade were each strapped to an experienced glider to soar over the earth, like a kite or bird. The sky was blue—puffs of idyllic white clouds—and below looked like a diorama, which in a way, to God, it was. Humans were the heads of pins, trees like green tufts of a wool sweater, and in the great blue ocean below, a bowl of water, surfboards floated like sprinkles. It was literally breathtaking: Ruby's head grew light and she reminded herself to inhale.

After that, they changed into rubbery black suits, strapped oxygen tanks to their backs, and slid their feet into flippers. The water that, only hours ago, appeared blank from a distance was rich with life: schools of shining fish, cityscapes of vibrant coral, marine animals that struck them as wearing expressions that were stoic, clownish, expectant, smug. Yes, it was anthropomorphizing, but why not engage in anthropomorphism this one final occasion? Jade and Ruby swam side by side, through curtains of gently waving seaweeds, each gesturing to capture the other's attention, to point out interesting fauna and flora to the other. It was all transcendently beautiful, Ruby thought. It wasn't that she was regretting her decision to be a freshwater turtle. But she was overcome with a feeling of awe. As Ruby swam, soundlessly beside her best friend amid the plethora of other creatures, she reluctantly conceded that God had done a pretty good job with the world. Quite honestly, it was possibly *too* good: too magnificent for any human to take in, too intricate, and improbable, and sublime. Maybe it was why human beings had the myopia they did, starting wars, committing atrocities against the planet and one another. Maybe it was why Ruby had spent so much of her humanity obsessing over what someone thought of her, or being annoyed with family members who voted for the wrong president, or reading arguments on Twitter. Humans were more at ease with human-size problems. Being struck with awe, remembering how small one was, how little one knew, the fact of one's mortality and insignificance and triviality—it was all deeply uncomfortable.

That evening, Ruby and Jade visited their families. In the front yard, Ruby hugged her father and her brother. Her mother was still too upset to speak with her, so Ruby left a handwritten note that she hoped sufficiently expressed how much she loved her.

～

Back at Ruby's house, they popped popcorn and watched *Chungking Express*. Over the years they'd found the film charming and then annoying and now charming again. They brushed and flossed their teeth not because they had to, but because sleeping with clean teeth felt nice. Lights out, lying side by side, they began to talk the way they had when they were girls having sleepovers. Earlier that day they had texted their final decisions to God, whale for Jade and turtle for Ruby, and received brown thumbs-up emojis.

At four in the morning, their time, all of humanity would evaporate. Each person would be transformed into the animal of their choice, placed in suitable habitats not of their choosing. It would happen painlessly, God assured, although what did God even know about pain? Ruby wondered. He experienced neither pain nor pleasure. He didn't know what it was like to have a best friend like Jade. *Poor God*, Ruby thought. Having a friend like Jade had been the best experience of her whole human life.

"Remember the time we raced snails?" Jade asked. Ruby could hear her smiling, in the dark. "And my mom got so mad because it was dinnertime. And the snails were too slow."

"I remember! And we brought them inside, in our pockets, to race in the bathtub."

"Delilah and Joseph."

"I can't believe you remember that. And one of them—I think it was mine—it died from fright before we reached the bathtub."

"I forgot about that. How terrible!"

"It's probably one of the reasons God is doing all this."

"That we're so careless with other animals?"

"Yeah. And with each other."

They lay in the silence for a long moment.

"Do you want to be conscious when this happens?" Ruby asked. "Or should we try to get some sleep?"

"I don't know. What about you?"

"I don't know, either."

There was another long silence.

"Jade, I'm sorry that—" Ruby paused.

There were so many things she needed to apologize for, she didn't even know where to begin. The times she'd neglected her friend because she believed her work was paramount. The times she'd been stubborn and hadn't compromised, when she easily could have to make Jade happy. The times she knew Jade was going through difficulties and Ruby hadn't known the right words to say. Despite being a writer she wasn't good with spoken words. During those periods she'd cooked bulk meals for Jade—tagines she'd lovingly prepared with lemons she'd preserved herself, or kimchi stews with kimchi she fermented—and mopped Jade's floor or taken out Jade's trash. She knew Jade would have liked to have been verbally reassured, but Ruby didn't have the right words to say. She never would, now.

"It's okay, Ruby." Jade's voice was clear and steady. "I know. I know you. I love you so much."

"I love you, Jade." Ruby reached out to take her friend's hand.

In the dark, they held hands, squeezing occasionally, until their hands grew unbearably sweaty, and each released the other at the same time.

"I don't think I can sleep," Jade said.

"Me, neither."

"Should we do something else?"

Ruby stood up and turned the lights on. She peeked out the window and saw that other lights were on, too.

"What about..." Ruby thought out loud. "What about YouTube karaoke?"

It was a perfect idea. Online, they could find almost any song in the world: lyrics presented against a backdrop of bizarre, often unrelated videos. The friends danced and laughed and sang at the top of their lungs to Tracy Chapman and the Cranberries and Macy Gray and Nirvana.

"Oh, I know!" Ruby exclaimed.

"What?" Jade asked.

"I have a good one. Hang on." Ruby angled her laptop away from Jade so that the song selection would be a surprise.

The familiar notes of Pachelbel's Canon in D came on. Jade broke into laughter, delighted. They didn't need the lyrics. The friends knew them by heart.

Ruby turned the lights back off and held her cellphone flashlight up, swaying with it as the chorus came on. Jade held hers up, too. They sang loudly about being friends forever, no matter what changes came.

"La, la, la, la, la, la, la, la, la, la," Ruby and Jade sang together, at the top of their lungs. "La, la, la, la, la, la, la, la, la, la—"

They put their phones down and, with their arms around each other's waists, were singing, as loudly as they had ever sung, when in a moment, a hundredth of a second, Ruby and Jade vaporized with the rest of humanity, atoms scattering, traveling, reassembling, to the Pacific Ocean for Jade and to a pond in Australia for Ruby.

But, as to be expected with such an enormous undertaking, there was a glitch. For a fraction of a second, Jade, in the body of a blue whale, and Ruby, in the body of a freshwater turtle, sustained human thoughts. Jade thought, *Ruby*, and Ruby thought, *Jade*. Then God put His divine palm to His divine face and corrected the error. From then on, Jade swam, and Ruby basked in the sun's warm rays.

And God looked upon everything that He had made, and behold, it was very good.

acknowledgments

I am grateful to my dear Marya Spence for ongoing support, compassion, and faith. I hope we get to work together till death do us part or the world ends, whichever comes first.

Thank you, John Freeman, for being the meticulous and huge-hearted editor of my dreams.

Thank you to the editors and copy editors who made these stories better: Lisa Borst, Cheston Knapp, Meg Storey, Jen Gann, Aimee Bender, Adam Dalva, Amy Ryan, John Freeman (again), Will Allison, and Patrick Ryan.

Thank you to all who helped transform this text into the book you are holding in your hands. I'm grateful to the hardworking teams at Knopf and Janklow and Nesbit, including but very much not limited to: Isabel Ribeiro, Mackenzie Williams, Jordan Pavlin, Kelly Shi, Erinn Hartman, Melissa Yoon, Linda Huang, Emily Murphy, Anna Knighton, Kathryn Ricigliano, Anne Achenbaum, Arianna Abdul, Sierra Fang-Horvath. Thank you also to the team at Hutchinson Heinemann: Amy Batley, Hana Sparkes, Laura Brooke, and others not listed here. Thank you, Michael Taeckens and Sarah Jean Grimm, for your specific magic.

Unending appreciation to the following humans, for feedback, in some cases, and friendship in all: Susanna Kwan, Meng Jin, Shruti Swamy, R. O. Kwon, Esmé Weijun Wang, Caille Millner, Colin Winnette, Andi Winnette, Margaret Wilkerson Sexton, Anisse Gross, Ingrid Rojas Contreras, Mimi Lok, Lauren Ro, Jessica Wang, Lexy Benaim, Aaron Thier.

Thanks to the San Francisco Arts Commission for the support that made several of these stories possible.

I owe a debt to various sources of inspiration, including the work of Aihwa Ong, especially "The Production of Possession: Spirits and the Multinational Corporation in Malaysia." CB Owens, for an unforgettable online dating anecdote. "Ghosting the Machine" by Sam Lipsyte. The National Coach Museum in Lisbon. Banner, Wyoming. Bunny, the best cat.

Thank you to my family: the Khongs, Tans, Horowitzes, and Kayes. Thank you, Eli, for more than can be included: love/forgiveness, snugs and puzz, our very good life.

A NOTE ABOUT THE AUTHOR

Rachel Khong is the author of *Goodbye, Vitamin*, winner of the California Book Award for First Fiction. *Real Americans*, her second novel, was a *New York Times* bestseller. In 2018, Khong founded The Ruby, a work and event space for women and nonbinary writers and artists in San Francisco's Mission District. With friends, she teaches creative writing in a collective called The Dream Side. She lives in Los Angeles.